MARKED BY FIRE

Praise for

MARKED BY FIRE

—ɯ—

Winner of the National Book Award

A New York Times *Notable Book of the Year*

"An abiding faith in the ultimate triumph of goodness . . .
a spiritual. . . . In *Marked by Fire*, the magic is still going on."
—*The New York Times Book Review*

". . . A story of remarkable depth, related in a hauntingly lyrical voice."
—*Publishers Weekly*

★"A lyrical celebration of black womanhood
tempered by both pain and joy."
—*Booklist* (starred review)

". . . An exquisite novel of life and death . . ."
—*The San Francisco Chronicle*

"This novel with its powerful character and beautiful language
is a testament to the strength of womanhood . . ."
—*Kliatt*

MARKED BY FIRE

by
Joyce Carol Thomas

Jump at the Sun
Hyperion
New York

*I dedicate this book to the memory
of my brother Roy Leon Haynes, M.D.,
doctor of medicine and of the spirit*

—J.C.T.

Published by Jump at the Sun/Hyperion Books for Children, an imprint of Disney
Book Group. No part of this book may be reproduced or transmitted in any form
or by any means, electronic or mechanical, including photocopying, recording, or
by any information storage and retrieval system, without written permission from
the publisher. For information address Hyperion Books for Children, 114 Fifth
Avenue, New York, New York 10011-5690.

First published in 1982 by Avon Books.
First Jump at the Sun edition, 2007
1 3 5 7 9 10 8 6 4 2
Library of Congress Cataloging-in-Publication Data on file.
Printed in the United States of America
This book is set in Adobe Caslon.
Designed by Ellice M. Lee

Hardcover edition:
Reinforced binding
ISBN-13: 978-1-4231-0143-7
ISBN-10: 1-4231-0143-X

Paperback edition:
ISBN-13: 978-1-4231-0144-4
ISBN-10: 1-4231-0144-8

Visit www.jumpatthesun.com

Acknowledgments

I am indebted to my ace editors, Kelli Martin and Colin Hosten, whose splendid comments always shimmer with light. I thank the Jump at the Sun/Hyperion Books for Children creative team for their affirmation and faith in publishing this 25th Anniversary edition of *Marked by Fire*.

I include here an acknowledgment of publisher, editor, and friend Joanna Cotler, who had the foresight and resolve to press Avon Books to publish the original edition of *Marked by Fire*.

I am appreciative also of Christine Earle, literary agent, for her brilliance and kindness.

I am grateful also to Bob Pimm for his early and gracious support of Abyssinia Jackson's continued journey.

As always, I am uplifted by encouragement from family, friends, librarians, teachers, literary critics, bookstore owners, and readers.

Thank you all for reminding me of my devotion to waking up every morning to write yet another page.

MARKED BY FIRE

Wednesday Morning

September 5, 1951

On a hill rise to the left of the cotton field, a hound dog howled woefully under a blackjack tree, his scruffy tail sticking out stiffly behind him. A string of chee-chee birds perched on the tree branches, the unborn song dying in their throats.

Patience looked up and saw the great whirling wind scoop down at the edge of the cotton field and yank up an entire row of ripe bolls and sturdy stalks.

Instinctively, her hands reached down and covered her watermelon belly. She felt the urge to run, but she knew she was too heavy. She was trapped there in the cotton patch, crouched on her knees, along with all the other workers. Her eyes followed the movement of the tornado as it ominously skipped and twirled along the boundaries of the field. She watched the tornado snap up the dog and listened, horrified, when his miserable howling ceased. She began to lift herself up on her knees.

"Daughter, don't move," Mother Barker in the next row whispered.

Patience sank back down on her knees and felt the sickness rising in her. There was no escaping it: the end was near.

In the row on the other side of Patience, Bessie Lightsey nervously sucked her fat thumb and tugged insistently at her mother's skirt. Mesmerized, she could not turn her eyes away from the tornado.

The dark spiral turned and headed toward them.

Patience gasped and clasped her hands together tightly. Mother Barker began to pray. In a muted voice, as though afraid the tornado might hear her, she prayed for deliverance.

"Lord, we know you know your business. We know we are but a speck of dust in the corner of your eye. But Heavenly Father, grant me permission to speak to you this morning, Sir. Now, Lord, you made the mountains. You made the forest and the streams."

She extended her hands toward Patience.

"Merciful Father, you even made the child your faithful handmaiden Patience is carrying.

"And Lord, you made the tornado, too. You made everything, including your humble servants.

"We understand you already predicted our comings and our goings. The hour and the minute of our birth. And Lord, if you wag your head on us you know the very second of our death. Father, if you wag your head on this unborn child, how can we watch it experience your wonderful light?

"Lord, we walk the earth at your command. Sir, if you willed it, in the twinkling of an eye we could be whipped away like a leaf before a treacherous storm. Lord, we're asking you to hold the tornado, and we're asking you to have mercy enough not to wag your head on us this morning."

The tornado picked up speed as it approached them. It turned and uprooted another row of cotton. The branches, leaves, and soft, white, downy fibers danced in its vicious and capricious clutch. Then, having satisfied its hunger, the tornado suddenly sailed away through the sky.

For a moment they stood completely frozen, silently holding their breath. When they were sure the twister had finally gone, Patience and the other women laughed nervously. The children whimpered. Mother Barker's husband, the foreman, and the only man in the field, adjusted his straw hat on his head.

Mother Barker stood up and smiled. "Wasn't that an amazing sight?" She surveyed the field. The mighty wind had swept a clean circle around them, leaving them untouched.

For a moment a line of worry wrinkled her forehead. She went over to Patience and placed her hands gently on the pregnant woman's stomach. "The baby's all right," Mother Barker announced with a sigh of relief.

"Look at my hands shake," said Patience.

"You might be upset naturally, but the baby's fine. This baby, I can tell, is going to be an Oklahoma wonder.

"Oklahoma!" Mother Barker hollered joyfully, her paisley head rag hanging halfway off her head. "You and your tornados and your rising river! We'll still be loving you, Oklahoma, till the rivers run out of water and the wind runs out of breath!"

Patience smiled at Mother Barker's exuberance. The older woman's presence was comforting. Assured that her baby was all right, she stopped her trembling and laughed along with Mother Barker.

"All right," the foreman proclaimed, measuring the remaining rows of cotton with his eyes. "Let's get back to work. We've got cotton to pick!"

Patience felt awkward getting up and down from the row of cotton. Her heaviness slowed her while the tight strap of the crocus sack cut into the long, muslin dress she had fashioned out of a flour bag. Now and then she shook her arm to relieve the dead feeling in her shoulder caused by the strap.

When Patience came to the end of her row, the foreman weighed her cotton on the hooked scale.

"Another fifty pounds! Believe you'll make two hundred before the day's gone."

"God willing," she answered.

"Two hundred pounds, I declare!" exclaimed Mother Barker. "I believe you'll beat me today," she said, picking alongside Patience.

"This cotton's so ripe you barely have to touch it. It just jumps in your sack."

Patience shaded her eyes and saw a cloud of chee-chee birds fly up on the east end of the field. Nothing else in the air stirred. The sun glared red-eyed and dropped heat on their bowed heads. Patience unbent herself and stretched, watching the brown chee-chee birds on the skinny, dark leaves of the miniature blackjack trees lift their wings and turn toward the sun. "I'd like to fly on away from here," she murmured. "Just like a bird. Only perch down to earth when I felt like it."

"I'm afraid you're too heavy to fly, child," Mother Barker allowed, looking at Patience's swollen belly.

5

When the sun had left, leaving only a rosy glow at the far end of the sky, the women pulled the long sack straps off their shoulders. They straightened up, put their hands on their hips, leaned back, and shook the cramps off their backs and legs.

The procession leaving the field that evening was colorful in look and sound. Bright scarves tied under their chins, bright sounds coming out of their mouths, the women marched toward the row of cabins on the field's edge, singing:

> *By and by when the morning comes,*
> *All the saints of God are gathering home.*
> *We will tell the story of how we overcome,*
> *And we'll understand it better by and by . . .*

They reached Patience's cabin first.

"Think I'll stir me up a little corn pudding this evening. Bring you some by after a while, with some greens and pot liquor. Pot liquor will give you strength," Mother Barker promised. "Think I'll fix a pot of broom wheat tea for you, too, because it'll sure help you rest good at night."

Inside her cabin Patience lit the oil lamp. Then she unhooked the bucket from the wall and walked to the well at the end of the cabins' path, swinging the bucket to the rhythm of her stride. On the way back she could no longer make out the white rows. The fields of cotton had blended with the night.

To take the chill away from the cold well water, she heated it on top of the wood stove. She then sloshed it across the floor and began scrubbing the planks with a stubby, bristled brush, carefully scouring between the splintered boards. She threw out pails of dirty water and pumped more fresh water from the well until the floor was clean of dust and grime.

She hung two morning-star quilts across the line, stretching them until they were taut, and then beat them with her broom, letting fresh air in through the patchwork. She took them back inside and plumped them on her bed.

She noticed that Mother Barker had placed the food she had promised on the stove. In a heavy, black-iron skillet, Patience fried cornbread on top of the stove, then sat down heavily and ate Mother Barker's corn pudding and greens seasoned with fatback. She sipped the warm broom wheat tea and gazed long into the fire.

And what would the baby be like, she wondered. She and her husband, Strong, had waited so hopefully for this child, the fruit of their marriage. She smiled to herself as she remembered Strong's face the day she told him they were going to have a child. His eyes lit up like stars. He danced her around the floor, and then sat her down carefully like she was rare, expensive, antique china. She missed him now, but they had agreed that she would go on to the harvest while he stayed in Ponca to mind his barbershop.

She remembered their courtship. Of all the men who had come courting when her father said she was of age, she had chosen Strong Jackson. Partly because he was ambitious—he had just opened the Better Way Barbershop—and partly because of his rich, deep laugh. He knew how to amuse her. His courtship talk had been smooth and colorful.

They had wed at the beginning of summer. Her sisters, Serena and Sadonia, were her bridesmaids. They had placed fresh cut flowers from the yard in jars and pots all over the newlyweds' cabin.

Patience closed her eyes and smelled the aroma of roses, jasmine, heather, hollyhock, aster. She took a deep breath, then opened her eyes and gazed again into the fire. The yellow flame reminded her of the brilliance of the wedding flowers.

Patience dozed by the fire. Her head began to fall to her chest.

She jerked awake. She got up and put a small pan of water on the table, then dipped her hands into the water and wet her face. Now plump beyond their usual chiseled sharpness, the angles of her face were soft and rounded. The high cheekbones curved more, and the formerly thin, jutting jawbone now sloped. She took a cloth off a nail, dipped it in water, and washed all over. She thought of how her body would be trim again when the baby finally came. How quickly and easily she would move! The water trickled down her naked face, cool as a spring breeze in a field of fragrant mint.

She climbed into the high bed, which she had warmed at the foot with hot bricks wrapped in flannel. So tired, tired from the cotton. The weariness and the tea worked their magic, and she fell into a deep, warm sleep.

Thursday Morning
September 6, 1951

When Patience awoke, the rooster had not crowed yet. The workers headed for the field just before sunrise. The foreman started a fire down by the bin, using dead wood he had gathered under the spreading trees. For kindling he used slivers of sticks and fallen twigs. The women clustered in a circle around the fire, rubbing their hands together, scanning the field, and picking out sets of rows with their eyes. All the while the acrid smoke, lifting itself toward the sky, filled air and stung the insides of their noses. Then the hungry flame stuck itself to the dried tinder and began eating up the wood. The flame ate and grew taller. When the fire was half as tall as they were, the women fanned out into the field. One by one they knelt down as though worshipping the cotton.

When the sun reached a quarter of the way across the sky, Patience tugged the crocus sack back along between the rows to the bin. As the foreman reached for it, she suddenly realized that the bag was the heaviest thing she had ever lifted. Perspiration was beading down her nose and soaking her armpits. She felt water running down her legs. Her mind wanted to stop the water, but it would not stop. She could not move; water stuck her to the spot. Water wet her cotton stockings and flooded over the tops of the laced-up shoes and down the dusty trail that the crocus sacks left on their way to the bin.

"Woman!" the foreman shouted at Mother Barker with male uneasiness. This was an area over which he had no authority. "Woman!"

Hearing the urgency in his voice, everybody in the field looked up, their bonnets pushed back from their brows. In the distance Patience saw the women standing like black stalks against the sky.

Mother Barker ran to the weighing-in area. Patience had not moved. One look at Patience's face and it was clear she would never make it back to the cabin in time.

The foreman's wife spoke softly. "Time."

More women came, throwing down their sacks between the fire and the bin, then hurriedly arranging the sacks into a great pallet. Onto this Patience was carefully settled, her legs spread-eagled. The foreman's wife began to hum a song they all knew, a song without words. One of the women took off her bonnet and fanned Patience.

The foreman added more kindling to the fire. His wife placed the water can for drinking over the flame, and soon you could hear the water bubbling under the chorus of humming.

"Won't be long," the foreman's wife promised.

Soon the humming turned into moaning, and Patience gritted her teeth.

"Wait. Breathe deep, daughter," someone said.

Now and then the humming, the moaning, and the gurgling water mingled until you could not tell where one started and the other stopped.

"Push hard, now."

"Help, mercy!"

The women hummed together like light coming together after the sun has risen noon high, while pain and wonder wrapped around each of them in the humming. And the pain sat down on Patience and smothered her.

"Oh, glory."

"Push."

Each woman felt the pain.

"Push."

Each woman felt the pain and wonder as old as time,

as old as the sound of the women themselves as they rocked together, humming. Who could push pain away?

"Breathe deep, more deeper."

"Push down. Harder, I say."

The pain crouched low, drew back, and struck Patience so hard that although it was noon, she felt God light the night with lightning and wake up the world with thunder. The pain slashed deeper still until it cut off her breath.

The foreman, bound by a rule as old as human life—that man should not see the mystery of birth for it would be like staring God in the face—left the women and walked toward the grove of blackjack trees. When he reached the grove's edge, he heard his wife say, "Hallelujah!" Then he heard the sound of a slap.

And Abyssinia screamed her way into the world, water on one side, fire on the other.

"Whose Child are you?"
"I am the daughter of patience and strength."

In Ponca City, in the cool of the evening, the older people invariably sat out on their porches to reiterate the events of the day. They wanted to witness all that went on with the neighbors. They were particularly interested in the new baby, Abyssinia. The women of Ponca City considered themselves midwives-in-common at her birth.

She filled their conversations.

"Remember it like it was only yesterday," one of them commented.

"Born in the cotton field."

"Came here marked, too."

"Marked by the fire!"

"Baptized with the fire!"

"Foreman built the fire."

"Boiled water for the birthing."

"Patience spread out on her pallet of cotton sacks."

"And here comes our baby."

"An ember jumped out of the blaze and branded the child."

"Marked at birth!"

"A birthmark."

"Placed the new child on a soft sack of cotton."

"Laid her in a cotton manger."

"A black girl in a manger."

The women sat rocking on their porches. They wanted to hear each other's version of what the new child meant.

Now and then the people could hear the cries coming from Patience and Strong's house. Baby Abyssinia was a special project for the Ponca City women.

From the window overlooking their yard, Patience held Abyssinia up to watch the seasons pass. The baby watched the changing seasons. In autumn the rustling orange leaves fluttered down to earth. In winter the pecan tree stood sparse and bare, its limbs all but cracking under the strain of ice and snow. When the wind blew through the sapless branches, the tree complained like an old woman complains of arthritis deep in her bones in winter.

Patience began the winter preparations. The awful-smelling asafetida bags were prepared to go around Abyssinia's neck. A crock jar of blackstrap molasses for strength and for the blood was set atop the kitchen shelf among the jars of dried crowder peas, cornmeal, coffee, and flour.

The women stopped by to visit the baby. They spoke a universal language—baby talk.

"Oh, you're so pretty," they purred to her.

"Sweetest doll in Oklahoma," Mother Barker whispered.

They examined the birthmark left on her cheek by the ember from the fire.

"Looks like a dusty rose," Serena, her aunt, cooed.

"It's a rose for sure," some said.

"No, it's in the shape of a cotton blossom," others commented.

Everybody held Abby. Some of the older, childless women begged Patience and Strong to let her spend the night with them so they could play mother to her, so they might leave their own impressions upon the baby's life. They made her dresses and her own special quilt from scraps.

Patience's sisters were so possessive of the baby that Strong sometimes felt superfluous.

This evening Patience went over to the baby bed to pick up Abby, but she was not there. Strong must have taken her for a walk, Patience thought.

But when he came home, his arms were empty. She asked, "Where's the baby?"

"Where's the baby? How would I know?"

"Stop playing, Strong."

"I'm not."

He looked over toward the empty baby bed. She realized he was as mystified as she was.

He said, "Maybe one of your sisters got her."

"Sadonia did come by yesterday asking to keep her, but I told her no."

"What does that mean to Sadonia? She comes in here and borrows your dresses and your hats without asking. What's to stop her from borrowing your baby?"

"A baby's not a dress or a hat."

"It sure isn't. But I bet you she got her. Let's go see."

They left the house and walked two doors down to the home of the two spinster sisters.

As they stepped up on the sisters' porch, they could hear Sadonia talking baby talk. Her voice was light and high.

"Now ain't that cute. Smile and show Mama your dimples now. Gicchy, gicchy, goo. Gicchy, gicchy, goo."

Patience turned the doorknob. Folks didn't lock their doors in Ponca City. The door would not budge.

"Gicchy, gicchy, goo. Gicchy, gicchy, goo."

Strong knocked on the door.

The baby talk abruptly stopped.

He knocked again.

Patience hollered, "Yoo-hoo, Sadonia? Serena?"

Nobody answered.

"Open the door!" Strong insisted.

No response.

He pounded harder on the door, bringing the curious neighbors out of their houses to wonder what all the commotion was about.

"I know you're in there. Open this door and give us our baby," demanded Strong.

"Yoo-hoo, Serena! Yoo-hoo, Sadonia!"

Finally Serena answered, "What do y'all want?"

"We want our baby," said Strong.

"She's not here," said Sadonia.

Strong got angrier. He pounded on the door. "You open this door now, or I'm calling the law!"

"We didn't do anything wrong!"

Patience said, "Open the door and stop acting crazy."

Strong rapped harder on the door. Abyssinia started to squall.

"I told you that baby was in there," Strong said to Patience.

"See there, you made the baby cry," screeched Serena, secure beyond her door.

"Get away from my door," said Sadonia.

"Baby snatchers!" accused Strong. "You've got some loony sisters," he said to Patience.

'Well, they won't hurt her," Patience said in defense of her sisters. "But I'm afraid her nursing time's near."

"Bring that baby out of there so this woman can nurse her," Strong hollered through the door.

The baby cried louder.

"We can feed her," said Sadonia.

"You don't have any milk," said Patience.

There was no response to that, but soon the squalling stopped. Patience squatted down by the front door and looked through the opening in the curtain of the window. She could see Sadonia trying to nurse Abyssinia. The baby's jaws were working. Sadonia was rocking and petting the baby. The baby was pacified.

"Come here, Strong, and look," Patience said.

Strong stooped over and looked, too. When he could make out the two figures, he rattled the window. "Woman, you open this door. You can't nurse a baby. Your titties are as dry as the desert."

"Get away from my door. You're disturbing the baby," said Sadonia.

"Serena," said Patience as an idea occurred to her, "I'll see you in church tonight." She started walking away from the porch.

"Woman, where are you going?"

"Home to get ready for church. Some gospel singers are coming from out of state tonight, don't you remember? Sadonia and Serena never missed church in all their life. Much as they enjoy gospel, they won't miss the service. We'll get the baby then."

"We'd better!" announced Strong angrily. He reluctantly turned away from the porch. "They're as crazy as Betsy bugs!"

At home Patience dressed carefully for church. She thought about how Abyssinia had become a bench baby. Patience would take her to church in her baby basket and leave her sleeping or awake, on the church bench. When she cried, there was always someone to hold her: one of her aunts or any of the surrogate aunts, uncles, grandmothers, and grandfathers who kept watch over her. It was not often that the baby cried, though, particularly during the music and singing portions of the service.

The baby felt the music in an immediate way. Spirituals lulled her to sleep, and church-rocking gospels roused her awake. When the chorus of certain songs was repeated, some folks claimed that Abby hummed along with the singers. Even Mother Barker, who was known for telling the truth, said it sounded like the baby was humming.

Everybody laughed. They were not sure just what it meant. One sister asked, "How can a baby come here singing?"

All Patience wanted to know was, "Did it sound like Abby was humming in tune?"

Dressed in their Sunday best, Patience and Strong walked to church. There was no sign of noise or movement coming from behind the closed door of her sisters' house.

"Who's singing tonight?" Strong asked her.

"The Five Blind Boys. They're on tour. Going all over the country. And the Dixie Hummingbirds, too."

The Five Blind Boys from Alabama were harmonizing when they reached the church. People were humming along with them. Some patted their feet in time to the singing. Others participated by waving their handkerchiefs. Patience and Strong sat down and listened. Patience kept turning around, looking at the door.

The Dixie Hummingbirds were next on the program, and they proceeded to tear up the church with their singing. People got so happy that they shouted, knocked over chairs, and even upset the collection table. Patience kept looking back at the church entrance.

She thought she heard a baby crying. Was it her baby? Brother Lightsey was shouting out of his shoes. His loud cries to the Lord muffled the sounds she thought she heard.

The Dixie Hummingbirds kept on singing. Patience listened to them with one ear. She was sure she heard a baby crying in her other ear. She turned around.

Into the church stepped Sadonia with the baby wrapped in a blanket. Serena followed behind her. The baby was crying louder now. It was a lusty, hungry cry. All the women recognized the infant's sound of hunger.

Sadonia deposited the baby in its basket on the bench and sat down with Serena in the front row.

Patience got up from her seat and went to the baby, picking her up. The hungry child smelled the milk from her mother's thick breasts and made smacking sounds with her mouth.

Patience returned to her seat and took a diaper out of her purse. She unbuttoned the top of her dress and covered her bosom with the diaper. She then commenced to nurse the child.

Abyssinia ceased her crying.

Once in a while when nap time for Abyssinia arrived, Mother Barker would come to Patience's porch and rock the baby to sleep. This afternoon she took Abby to her own house to let the tot watch her administer folk medicine to the women wrapped in shawls who came calling at her doorstep. Some days Mother Barker would get the child back home just in time for her to stand on her own porch and wave her father home. The image that greeted Strong was that of a warm, chocolate girl holding on to the porch rail in a starched dress with a bow tied in the back and a ribbon dancing on her head. Moonstones sparkled in her dark, black eyes. He thought about the velvet interiors of pansies when he watched her smile and say the simple word, "Daddy."

Inside the Jackson house, in her mother's arms, Abyssinia again watched the snow falling like chilled confetti out of the Oklahoma sky. As the year progressed, the white coldness turned brown and melted, the birds came back singing the same hopeful songs. Patience's asafetida bag was strongly aromatic when it hung around Abyssinia's neck in winter; as spring came, the bag lost its pungency and was discarded. A cow had a calf in the ongoing circle of creation. Before long it was August again.

Soon after Abby began to take her first steps, Mother Barker took her walking in the country through pastures of unfenced fields. She took Abyssinia on nature walks, hunting certain roots and leaves and specific barks on trees. She would spy a plant and say, "Abby, pull that root up and bring it here."

Abyssinia would stoop over, and with her small child's hands, she'd dig the plant loose from the soil and offer the greenery to Mother Barker. "No, that's not it."

They searched a short distance farther. "Wait a minute. Pull this one up . . . gently now." The old woman peered at the new discovery, turning it over in her hand. "That's not it either," she said. Stooping down, she put the plant's root safely back in its home of soil.

Mother Barker walked with her head bent toward the

ground, like a bird searching for worms, seeing what Abby could not see.

"Stop, stop, stop, Abyssinia! Hand me that there piece here. Yes, this is it all right." And a smile wrinkled the corners of her eyes. "This is the one, all right." She gave the child a kiss on her cotton-blossom birthmark.

And she put the plant in a rough fabric bag. Taking Abyssinia's hand, she hummed softly to herself as they struck out for home.

*"I washed my face with
the velvet cloth of laughter."*

Abby looked forward to going to the Better Way
Barbershop. She liked to sit and listen to the yarns the men
spun, especially the stories her father told. He promised to
take her with him on her fourth birthday.

Patience had dressed her in ribbons and a Sunday-go-
to-meeting yellow dress.

"What color icing do you want on your cake, Abby?"

"Pink, Mama."

Patience—through magic, Abby thought—could turn
a birthday cake into some color other than the regular
white frosting she used to decorate the Sunday cakes. She
could color it green or pink or bright yellow. Patience had
already begun to whip the cake batter when Abby's father
took her hand and headed for the door.

They stopped by the store where he bought her a coloring book. When they got to the Better Way, he sat her down in the front of the shop.

"Having my pretty daughter here is better than having a bowl of flowers in the place."

"Now that's a fact," the men agreed.

"She can sit in that chair for hours coloring her pictures and won't get in my way at all. She's not one of those whining children who never let their folks have a drop of peace. That's my Abby," he boasted.

What Abby liked best about her father was his sense of humor. He even laughed and poked fun at himself. The men came from miles away to get their hair trimmed and to listen to the stories that fell from the mouth of the barber.

Abby's father used to say that because he was bald-headed, people wouldn't look at his head to judge how theirs would look when he finished cutting.

The Better Way Barbershop was an institution on the black side of Ponca City. Like all institutions, it had its regular members. Even the winos looked upon the Better Way Barbershop as their meeting point. With flaming eyes they stood on the corner outside the building and made momentous decisions about what the president's next move was going to be. When the weather got ugly, they drained their Thunderbird bottles, tossed them in the trash, and moved inside.

The reverend from the Solid Rock Church of God in Christ came to the Better Way and left his unwanted hair along with the title of the next Sunday sermon. The colored taxicab driver came and mentioned that Leon Brown's wife, Ida, had packed up and left town.

Abby's father was not above telling a joke about himself, knowing how it would run through the town like one of those Oklahoma tornados. He liked to keep his shop lively.

"That's my baby," he said, proudly referring to Abby. "Today's her birthday. Born four years ago today. Reminds me of something that happened when she wasn't but a few weeks old. Something between me and her mother, but the baby was in the middle of it."

Abby's father shook out the barber bib as he beckoned the reverend to the chair.

He began, "They say, if you put a pea under a mattress, a queen can feel the bump in the bed and will scream holy murder. And if you pile ten mattresses on top of that one, the queen will still feel the bump. So it is with a black woman. She knows when something's not right. She's not evil, she's queenly."

He launched into the story proper. "Now I knew Patience was up to something. She was too nice. Had fixed my favorite food—barbecued ribs, string beans and new potatoes, a mess of greens, with a saucer of sliced onion marinated in vinegar on the side. She'd baked my favorite chocolate cake and had my coffee creamed till it was light brown, like she is. I knew she was being too nice. Had dressed the baby up in something pretty made out of ribbons."

Abby's father lathered the reverend's face like he was frosting a cake and tilted his customer's chin back with his thumb. He looked over at Abby and asked her if she wanted to get herself some red soda water. Abby shook her head. She didn't want to miss the story.

Strong continued the tale, "Like I said, she had dressed the baby up in something pretty she had made out of ribbons. Wanted us to take Abby by her sisters', so she could go out on the town with me Saturday night.

"I said, 'No, honey.'" Strong scraped away the white cream from the reverend's face and surveyed the barbershop brotherhood. "Taking a wife to a party would've been like taking bologna to a barbecue.

"Now that woman can get 'evil' in a hurry. Something funny happens to her eyes, and her mouth, it gets shut like a trap."

"You mean queenly, don't you?" the reverend reminded him.

"Yeah, that's right. Can get real queenly, right quick. 'Patience,' I told her, 'now you know it's not good for a new baby to be out in the open air at nighttime.' Told her this while I was shining my alligator shoes.

"'Patience,' I said, 'a good-looking woman like you could get a man in all kind of trouble. Why, if some hardhead looked at you too long, I'd have to ask him outside. And you know you don't like me fighting, baby.' I said this to her while I was brushing off my mohair suit. All the time hot embers were building up in her eyes. Jaws were tight."

Strong paused, shaking the razor blade for emphasis. "I was drawing my bathwater, understand? And steady talking to her.

"I said, 'Patience, sweetheart, a man can't take a good-looking woman like you in among any and everybody. Even the Bible says, "Cast not your pearls down before swine."

"'Honey,' I said, 'could you scrub my back? Woo, that feels good! Go up just a little bit, more to the right. You almost got it. Just a little higher. Yeah! Right there. That's it.' You know, a woman is something else."

Strong started snipping the top of the reverend's hair. Abby noticed that it had started raining outside. The barbershop was beginning to fill up. Her father became more animated.

"Then she went to tend to my baby Abby while I just lay back in that tub and soaked and soaked and soaked. Man, there's nothing like an old-fashioned Saturday night bath.

"'Patience, honey, hand me a towel,' I ordered. She brought me this big, fluffy, man-size towel, kind of watermelon colored. She even dried my back. Now I knew she was feeling better, her jaws had gotten a little slacker. Her eyes sparkled that magic, merry way they can do sometimes."

Strong looked up from the reverend's head. He nodded as another regular customer walked into the barbershop.

"Didn't even fuss at me about cleaning out the bathtub like she usually would. She got down on her knees and scrubbed the tub out herself.

"'You're a sweet woman,' I said.

"Man, let me tell you. My woman had laid out my brown socks to match my brown mohair suit. My woman got my handkerchief and folded it catty-cornered in my suit pocket. My woman sprinkled some sweet-smelling Three Roses all over my jacket. Talk about sharp!"

Strong stepped back for a long look at both sides of the reverend's head. Satisfied, he resumed clipping.

"Pecked her on the cheeks as I stepped out the door.

Was saving my kissing for later on. Had more interesting things for my lips to do, you understand.

"Stuck my wedding band in my pocket and went to the party. The women there!" Strong rolled his eyes. "Chocolate-drop beauties! Caramel-colored wonders! Cinnamon babies! Nutmeg numbers! They had all the women!"

"What you say!" the winos commented.

"Well, I picked out this apricot, light-skinned chick. Had some legs on her big as Georgia hams. Talk about shapely!"

Strong licked his lips. "Had hips from here to that front door. That woman was fine! I started my rap, said,

Baby, when God made you,
He made a wonder.
He didn't make lightnin'
Without the thunder.
He made all beauty
That men should see.
When He made you
He was thinkin 'bout me!"

Strong paused here and smiled, remembering his smooth line.

"She grinned and flashed her gold teeth, and we started dancing. We did the jitterbug, the cha-cha-cha, the strut. Every time the band struck up, we hit the floor.

"Man, I was the envy of the party, and I was thinking about polishing off the evening, dancing the night away with that lady on the ballroom floor. Just thinking about it made me excited, so I started perspiring a little bit."

"It was time to sweat all right," one wino commented.

"Like I say," Abby's father continued, "I started perspiring. Reached in my mohair suit pocket for my handkerchief to mop my brow . . . and unfurled a baby diaper big as a sheet across my face!"

"A baby diaper?" the reverend asked, sitting up in the chair as Strong untied the bib from around his neck. The barbershop brotherhood broke loose laughing. The laughter tingled Abyssinia down her spine and to her toes.

Strong shook his head, remembering the occasion. "Patience had pressed and ironed one of Abby's soft diapers just so and folded it in little tiny squares until it was no bigger than a handkerchief. There I was, the life of the party, strutting proud with a baby diaper in my suit pocket!"

Saturday Afternoon
July 1, 1961

---

*"I sat before the fire of a woman who
kept her fingers on the pulse of the wind."*

Generally, Abyssinia and the other children played in the backyards of Ponca City where all the washing was hung out on one day, where the vegetable garden was cultivated and harvested, where the chickens were fed, and—for the fortunate—where there was a tree old enough to support a swing.

The door leading from the kitchen to the backyard was left open so that Patience could watch Abby and her best friend, Lily Norene, while overseeing the washing and preparing homemade peach ice cream.

Patience scalded the milk, then jabbed the ice pick into the big crystal hunk of ice that weighed several pounds. She broke the ice into small chunks, which she packed around the ice cream barrel with handfuls of rock salt.

"Miss Jackson, Abby won't let me have my turn," Lily Norene complained. The argument was over who would turn the crank on the ice-cream churn. Lily Norene stood with her mouth poked out. She was a high yellow, broad-nosed little girl with lips like two perfect bows.

"Abby—oh, Abby, y'all share."

"Yes, Mama."

"Lily, I'll count to a hundred while you crank. Then it's my turn and you can count, okay?"

Once Lily Norene had agreed in a voice loud enough for Patience to hear, Abby began to race through the numbers faster than Lily could crank. ". . . One hundred. My turn."

The neighbor's daughter reluctantly surrendered the churn.

Patience let the screen door slam behind her as she went outside to hang more clothes. She shook out each piece and pinned it neatly on the line. She hung the towels all together. She pinned the shirts in one row and the dresses in another row.

When the cranking of the ice-cream churn became difficult, Abby began to count more slowly while Lily turned. Patience realized the ice cream must be ready.

"You can stop now," she called to the girls.

Abyssinia went to the kitchen and brought out two

dishes and two spoons. She pried the cold lid off the top of the churn and spooned nearly equal mounds of the delicacy into the dishes for herself and her friend. They sat on the back steps and enjoyed the rich, cool thrill of ice cream on their tongues and down their throats. The sweet peach smell hung pleasantly in the hot, still air.

When Patience finally heard the vigorous scraping of spoons against the bottom of the dish, she called, "Abyssinia, I want you to go over to Mother Barker's and read the *Black Dispatch* for her, you hear?"

"Yes, ma'am." The two girls rinsed the dishes in the sink, dried them, and put them back on the kitchen shelf.

"Can you come with me, Lily?" Abby asked.

"No, my mama says I can't go off the block."

"Oh, come on, Lily. You can at least walk with me a little way."

"Okay . . . but . . . I can't go far."

"All right."

"You always get to go over to Mother Barker's to read."

"Yeah. Sometimes it's fun, but sometimes I like to be by myself. Everybody's always watching me."

"I know," said Lily.

"I can't get away with anything," complained Abby.

The two girls took the path behind the schoolhouse. They walked slowly, listening to the bubbling sound of the

Ponca Creek, now alive with minnows, leaping frogs, and grasshoppers.

"It's good to be out of school," said Lily.

"Yeah, I heard Mother Barker say the cotton must be almost high."

The path followed the creek closely, beneath mulberry trees and thickets of rambling blackberry.

Now and then Abby would glance through the leaves of the mulberry trees into a Ponca City backyard where a vegetable garden would be flourishing. The yards were separated by hedges and natural fences of rambling roses.

"I think I'll climb that tree," Abby said to Lily.

"You're asking for trouble," Lily warned.

"No, I'm not. Anyway, I get tired of being good all the time. I feel like climbing that tree, and I'm climbing that tree."

"I'm going home," said Lily. "I wasn't even supposed to come this far."

"Go ahead then, scaredy-cat."

"I am not a scaredy-cat!"

"Yes, you are. Scaredy-cat, scaredy-cat, scaredy-cat!"

"You're just bad. I'm telling. Anyway my mama's showing me how to bake a cake today. That's something you don't know how to do, even if you do always get to read to Old Mother Barker. I'm baking a cake, ha, ha, ha!"

Lily stuck out her tongue and wagged her finger in Abby's face. Abby grabbed Lily's finger and bit it.

"Oh, oh, oh!" wailed Lily, crying. She started running for home.

Abby unlaced her shoes and climbed the tree where she looked down on the backyards of the colored part of town. They reminded her of a picturesque quilt, these various irregular-shaped plots of land. The inside of the patches bloomed a pattern of crinkly lettuce, lush collards and mustards, long green beans, succulent yellow corn, and juicy red tomatoes. The natural fences of rambling roses, heather hedges, and crawling vines formed the seams of the quilt.

Her attention focused on the yard just beneath her, the Lightseys' place. She saw none of the thirteen boys and girls who made up the household. They must be over at the school playground, Abby thought.

Abyssinia climbed down out of the tree into the back-yard. The sight of the vegetables had whetted her appetite. She reached down into the green vines and pulled out a tomato. She sat down on the edge of the row and ate the fresh red fruit, wishing she had some salt. She pulled off an ear of corn and had just taken her first big bite when she saw Sister Lightsey start out her back door with a basket of clothes to hang on the line. Sister Lightsey, a big, brown-skinned woman, saw Abby and stopped still.

"Girl, what do you think you're doing in this backyard?"

"Nothing."

"Does your mama know you're over here?"

"No, ma'am."

"You haven't asked me for anything?"

"No, ma'am."

"Where're you supposed to be?"

"Over to Mother Barker's."

"Come here, Abby." Sister Lightsey headed for the mulberry tree.

"Ma'am?" Abby backed away. She knew what Sister Lightsey was up to.

Sister Lightsey reached up and pulled a limb off the tree. Then she pulled another one down and began to braid the switch.

Abby backed away.

"Don't you run from me. You know if you run, you get two whippings."

Abby wanted to run, and she wanted to stay. If she ran, she was in trouble. If she stayed, she was in trouble.

Sister Lightsey stung the child's legs with the switch. Abby broke into a run around the garden, the grown-up and the switch in pursuit. Sister Lightsey kept stinging her legs, sending Abby skipping through the tomatoes, the corn, the cucumbers, and the greens.

When Sister Lightsey felt she had done her duty, she asked Abby again, "Now where're you supposed to be?"

"Over to Mother Barker's," Abby sniffed.

"Well, I think you'd better hurry along."

Abby scurried up the tree and dropped back down to the other side of the hedge. She resumed her trek along the path by the creek. She tried to remember what Patience had once told her: "Only those who love you can give you whippings." It seemed to her that the whole town knew her every step. They stood her in corners and switched her good whenever she "needed" it.

But the townsfolk talked about Abby in a prideful way, too. The mothers of the church claimed she could recite by heart whole chapters from the Book of Psalms. On various afternoons Abby would be summoned to read the *Black Dispatch* to older people like Mother Barker, whose eyes had seen too much already.

Abyssinia finally reached Mother Barker's porch. The old woman was waiting for her. She smiled at Abby, taking in the switch scratches on her legs.

"What took you so long?" she asked.

"I was talking with that slow Lily."

"Where is she?"

"I guess she's at home."

"Why'd she go back home?"

"She had to. Her mama didn't want her to leave."

"Is that the only reason?"

"No."

"What then?"

"I bit her."

"You know you got a whipping waiting on you at home, don't you?"

"Yes, ma'am."

Mother Barker handed her the newspaper.

"How come you bit her?"

"Oh, she was bragging about how she was learning to bake a cake while I come to read to you."

"Uh-huh," said Mother Barker.

Abby scanned the newspaper for events that might be interesting to the older woman. "Mother Barker, it says here that over in Ardmore the police shot another black man. Name of Teddy Walker."

"That's a shame. Read on, daughter."

Abby noted, as she read on, that it was called justifiable homicide. She could not fathom why they would call it justifiable until she got to the end of the article when mention was made that the police thought the victim was brandishing a gun. However, no gun was found.

"Well," grumbled Mother Barker, "they won't even say what happened to the dead man's family. There's some things that never get recorded."

"What's that, Mother Barker?"

"Nothing, child." She turned her gray head away and looked off into the distance as if she were seeing something. Then she turned again to Abyssinia.

"Daughter, I think I'll show you how to bake a pound cake. In time for the church anniversary."

"Yes, ma'am."

"I do believe I will."

The church anniversary was an annual affair celebrating the date when the cornerstone was first laid. It was customarily held near the church grounds. Every year the street in front of the church was unofficially blocked from cars and roller skates and bicycles, the reverence of the occasion being respected by sinners and saints alike. Pots and platters of food were carried onto the porches of neighboring congregation members and set up on long tables covered with embroidered cloths.

The reputations of the town's cooks were at stake, and they blessed the tables with the lightest cakes, the flakiest crusted pies, the tenderest chicken, and the most highly seasoned greens, buttered okra, succulent peas, and spicy potato salad, the fluffiest rolls, and the tastiest buttermilk cornbread. Not only was each woman's culinary craft on trial but also the good name of the church and of the town itself. Visitors came from all over the state, and occasionally a few filtered in from out of state.

"What will you be wearing, Abby?" Mother Barker asked.

"Mama's making me something."

"What color?"

"Blue. The prettiest blue."

"Child, did you know blue is the color of the will of God? Is she about finished?"

"Not quite. But it's got puffed sleeves that stop above my elbow. White lace around the sleeve edges. It's got a high collar with glass buttons running from the neck to the hem."

"Sounds like you're gonna be one precious-looking child."

"Yes, ma'am."

Abby knew what Mother Barker would be wearing. All the mothers of the church wore white uniforms with white gloves and white shoes and white hats.

"And what about your shoes?"

"Same as last year. Black patent leather."

"My, my, my." Mother Barker smiled. She looked Abby up and down, measuring the girl with her eyes.

"Yeah, I think we ought to teach you how to fix that pound cake for the anniversary."

Would she? Abby held her breath and wondered.

"Go across to Brother Jacobs and tell him to send me a pail of that good milk from one of his Guernsey cows, Abby."

With excitement rushing the blood to her head, Abby took her leave. She controlled the urge to run and shout. Mother Barker had never given out her secret recipe for pound cake. The cakes baked by the other mothers in the church never quite came up to Mother Barker's. Mother Barker would comment soundly but not maliciously, "Just because you've got the recipe, don't mean you've got the cake."

Abby was going to be given something nobody else had: the recipe and the cake!

The afternoon sun was a white fire in the sky, and perspiration beaded down Abby's forehead and trickled down under her armpits. The road parched the bottoms of her feet.

In the red barn behind the neat, white, wooden-framed house, Brother Jacobs in Uncle Ben coveralls was scooping cream off the milk and dumping it into a smaller pail. A tall, carrot-colored man with nappy red hair, he looked at Abby.

"Is Mother Barker fixing one of her cakes?"

"No, sir," Abby proudly revealed. "She's teaching me how. I'm getting practice so when anniversary day comes, I'll fix it all by myself."

Brother Jacobs nodded his understanding. "Here's one extra pail of milk for you. Save it for when you make your very own pound cake. You bring me a piece when you bring back these pails, you hear?"

The return to Mother Barker's was a much longer trip with the pails dangling carefully from her skinny arms. In spite of her cautiousness, she spilled a little milk.

She climbed the steps to Mother Barker's porch where the older woman still sat, rocking in the wooden swing.

"Go to the kitchen and pour yourself a glass of milk, child. Then get a Mason jar from under the sink and scoop the cream off the top of the milk into the jar.

"Then come on back outside here with the jar. Oh, yeah, put a top on the jar when you're through putting the cream in it."

Abby did as she was told and brought the jar of cream to Mother Barker who sat in the shade of the front porch and shook the jar of cream until yellow flecks of butter appeared through the glass. She gave the jar to Abby, who continued the vigorous shaking until the flecks grew into golden lumps of butter.

Mother Barker stood up. "Let's go into the kitchen," she said.

In the kitchen Mother Barker took out a huge crock bowl and a wooden spoon; she brought out the flour and the vanilla beans and a bowl of yard eggs. She told Abyssinia to put the canister of sugar on the table with the other items.

The private lesson took an hour and required neither pencil nor paper: it was essential that Abby keep all the information in her head. Mother Barker cautioned that it was not the ingredients alone, but how they were put together that made the difference.

"What did you taste in the kitchens of life?"
"Sometimes the wonderful red juice of the berry . . .
And sometimes the hull and peel of a bitter fruit."

"Lift every voice and sing/Till earth and heaven ring/Ring with the harmonies of liberty . . ."

The entire Attucks summer school student body assembled in the auditorium joined in the song. On one side of Abyssinia stood her best friend, Lily Norene. On her other side was her teacher, Miss Pat. Miss Pat sang the "Negro National Anthem" proudly, the red rose pinned to the bosom of her green dress heaving with each breath. Her student, Abby Jackson, was going to receive the Library Award for the most books read for her grade.

Abyssinia sang softly and fingered her newly pressed braids and bangs. She remembered yesterday's initiation into straightened hair. Her mother had taken down her small braids and washed and towel-dried her hair. The kiss of the hot comb that followed was unpleasantly close to the scalp. Looking at herself in the mirror afterward, Abby admired the two flat braids that had replaced the small tight ones she had had before.

"Let our rejoicing rise/High as the listening skies . . ."

As the song ended, the principal, bald-headed Mr. Mosely, walked to the podium. A short, stubby man, he wore a three-piece wool suit and bifocal eyeglasses. Mr. Mosely frowned perpetually. Even when he was smiling, he still looked like he was frowning.

"He ain't ugly, he's just original looking," Abyssinia said, nudging Lily.

They started to giggle, but Miss Pat gave them a stern look.

"We are proud today," Principal Mosely began, "to announce that we have awards to give to our most worthy students." He cleared his throat.

He talks like he's got marbles in his mouth, Abyssinia thought. He tied r's to the ends of his words.

"And we are gathered together here," he continued, "students and faculty of Attucks School, to honor these most worthy young scholars. And worthy they are. Worthy to be standing in these hallowed halls. Worthy to be students of Attucks, the school named for that most exemplary American, Crispus Attucks, first man to die in the American Revolution. And he was a colored man. We do Crispus Attucks proud today. We do our race proud today."

The principal shuffled his papers and cleared his throat. He looked at the trophies lined up before him.

"For the student who achieved the highest score in mathematics, Master Dexter Lightsey."

Dexter walked up to the podium and accepted the brass-plated trophy. He stepped to the microphone.

"My special thanks to my parents, to my brothers and sisters, to God, and of course to my teacher." Dexter took a deep bow and returned to his seat, his face flushed from the attention and the applause.

"Next, selected for the honor of most mannerly student, Miss Lily Norene Washington."

Lily could not hide her smile of pleasure as she walked up to Mr. Mosley. As he contemplated her beaming face, it occurred to him to embark on a longer speech.

"As recipient of the award for the most mannerly student in her grade, Lily Norene has conducted herself as a lady, paying honor to her elders and treating her fellow students with respect. It is she who rises when the teacher enters the classroom. It is she who pays attention and speaks only when spoken to. She is the example and beacon of politeness to all who pass within these Attucks walls. To you, Lily Norene Washington, this award."

Lily graciously accepted the small shining trophy and walked back down the aisle to her chair.

The principal looked over to Abby and began to speak.

"This next award is the award most special to my heart. A race is judged by its literacy, the ability of its members to read. The young lady I'm about to call up here not only has read just about every book in the library, but when school is out, she goes around town and reads to the elderly and shut-ins. This habit of reading is indeed most wonderful. Her teacher, Miss Pat, has given me a list of the books this student has read. I'll share a few titles with you: *Gulliver's Travels, Alice in Wonderland, The Wizard of Oz, Little Women* . . . Miss Abyssinia. . . ."

Abyssinia started to stand when the school bell began to clang. Mr. Mosely stopped talking. The students moved restlessly in their seats.

"Tornado," somebody whispered.

"Tornado!"

Mr. Mosely quickly folded the paper on which he had written the awards and stuck it in his pocket.

"We will quietly file down to the storm cellar. In order. In order," he said.

Both students and staff lined up and filed down to the basement. Whenever the word "tornado" buzzed through the line, Mr. Mosely admonished, "There will be no talking."

In the cellar they played spelling-bee games and tic-tac-toe. They recited Paul Laurence Dunbar poems and told ghost stories.

Three hours later, they emerged from the dark cellar into the open air. The entire student body stood gaping in awe.

A giant broom had swept a clean path through the world. There was virgin earth where houses, cars, and cattle had once been. Some structures had been leveled to the bare foundation.

"Look over there!" said Lily Norene. Abyssinia followed the direction of Lily's finger and saw Miss Sally hiding behind a tree. The two girls walked toward her.

Miss Sally grabbed Abby by the wrist and held on tight. The woman's eyes were two raccoon rings of terror.

"I saw it! I saw it, Abby," she said, her voice shaking.

"What, Miss Sally?" Abby asked.

"I saw the wind," she answered.

"The wind?"

"I saw the wind. Picked up the house." She halted. Abyssinia and Lily looked toward Miss Sally's house. The space where the house had been was empty.

"Lord," said Miss Sally, "it picked up the house and took it on up in the sky!" She held her ears. "It sounded like a whip whipping through the air."

"A whip, Miss Sally?" asked Abby.

"Yeah, and it almost got a hold of me."

Miss Sally tapped her head. Bushy, twisted black ropes of hair were scattered this way and that over her scalp. The two girls looked down at Miss Sally's legs. They were ashy now, as if the wind had whipped all the cold cream off them.

"How'd you happen to be in it, Miss Sally?" asked Lily.

"Child, I was on my way home to my cellar when I saw it. It was right up on my house. And once I saw it, I couldn't turn away. The sound of it caught me, and I couldn't move. And when it started to twisting and twirling and dancing its way over to my house, I stopped breathing. I stood by the blackjack tree . . . and . . ." Her eyes widened into large saucers, and she began to tremble.

Abyssinia started walking with Miss Sally. "Come on, Miss Sally," she said. Holding the terrified woman's trembling hand, Abby led her to Mother Barker's house.

"Mother Barker will know what to do," Abby told Lily.

Mother Barker examined Miss Sally carefully. She said a blackjack leaf went through Miss Sally when the big wind peeled the planks, one by one, off Miss Sally's old frame house and tossed them to the storm like brown sticks. She said the tornado took the handle off the iron tub and left the cow eyeless and gave Miss Sally the trembles.

"Not a thing more I can do," she said, shaking her head.

"Wonder why Mother Barker couldn't stop her trembling?" Abby asked Lily Norene as they walked home arm in arm.

"I don't know," said Lily.

"I guess we didn't help her much, did we?" Abby felt she had failed Sally.

"No, I guess not," said Lily.

The two girls had reached Abby's house. Abby hurried in. As she closed the door, she heard her mother talking to her Aunt Serena.

"It tore down the Better Way?" asked Patience.

"I saw it with my own eyes! I didn't see the tornado, but I saw the damage it did."

"You'd think he would have come home."

"No, he's out there babbling like a madman."

"Not Strong. Not my Strong."

"Crazy as a Betsy bug, I tell you. Your old man is crazy."

"Maybe he had too much to drink. . . ."

"Didn't have liquor on his breath. He's out there blaspheming. Said there's no such thing as God. Crazy, I tell you!"

"Strong wouldn't say that."

"Maybe the Strong you knew before the tornado wouldn't, but I saw the words falling out of his mouth myself. His eyes . . . his eyes looked crazy too."

"That shop was his life," Patience said, taking off her apron. "I'm going to look for him."

"Help yourself," said Serena. "The man has gone nuts."

"Where'd you see him last?" she asked.

"Saw him walking with Sally. Saw the two of them walking down the road together. She was trembling real bad . . . Sally . . . Trembling Sally."

"Oh, Mama, let's go get Daddy," Abyssinia cried.

"I must find him," her mother answered. "Abyssinia, you stay here. In case he comes this way before I find him."

"Yes, ma'am."

Abby stayed up for a long time after her mother had gone and it had gotten dark. She jumped up from her chair by the window now and then to look out the front door to see if her parents were coming home. At last she climbed in bed, but she could not sleep. Weary and alone, from her bed she watched the moon's silvery crescent on the night's horizon. When she heard the rooster's crowing, she watched the silver moonlight get blotted out by the bright blue of morning.

Then she heard the screen door open and slam. She

recognized the fall of her mother's steps, but she did not hear her father's heavier steps.

For the first time in her life, Abby was truly afraid. She felt uncentered. As long as she could remember, she had been waking up to the wonderful ring of her father's baritone voice, to her mother's tinkling soprano, to the calm, reassuring duet of her parents' conversations interspersed every now and then with an "Abby, are you up yet?"

Now that was changed.

She heard her mother's footsteps dragging across the living room floor. Abby's eyes felt like they had grains of sand in them. A strange wind roared in her head. She bounded out of the bed, pulled on her robe, and hurried to the living room.

"Mama, did you find him?"

"Abby . . ." She wrung her hands. "I mean . . ."

And they were in each other's arms sobbing, comforting one another.

"He'll be back, honey," her mother assured her.

Abby worried that perhaps this was something that neither her mother's love for her father, nor her father's love for her mother could remedy. She suspected it was like what happened to Miss Sally. There were some things even love or Mother Barker could not make right.

Abby said, "Oh, Mama, I wonder where he could

be? If we could just find him, I know . . ."

Her mother cut her off. "I don't know." Patience began wringing her hands more desperately.

"What is it, Mama?"

"I did see your daddy."

"But I thought you didn't find him."

"I saw him, but you see, he wasn't himself. I talked to him, but he wasn't listening. Then I just sat with him all night, not saying anything."

"Where was he?" Abby asked.

"Sitting where the barbershop used to be."

"Can I go see him?"

"It wouldn't do any good." Her mother started pacing the floor.

"Please?"

"Oh, Abby." A new wave of sobs overtook her. "I couldn't get him to come home!" Her shoulders drooped. Defeated, she sank into one of the chairs by the kitchen table.

"Mama, I want to talk to him. I want to see him."

Abby dashed out of the kitchen and out the front door on her way to where the Better Way Barbershop used to stand.

She told herself her father loved her.

"My father loves me, my father loves me, my father

loves me." She repeated the words faster and faster and faster.

But when she got to where the barbershop used to be, he was not there anymore. He was nowhere near where the Better Way had been.

"Have you seen my father?" she asked one of the men who stood on the corner every morning.

"No, Abby, I saw him earlier, but now I don't know where he is."

"Have you seen my father?" she asked the man in the grocery store.

"A little while ago."

"Have you seen my father?" she asked the paperboy.

"I saw him going down by the bus station."

"How long ago?"

"Not too long ago."

She dashed off in the direction of the bus station. Her feet were light. She was not conscious at first of her movement or her breathing. When she finally thought she would run out of breath, she rounded the corner to the bus station.

She saw a bus pulling out. She looked around the station quickly. Not seeing her father, she peered more closely at the moving bus. She recognized the back of her father's head in the row of seats.

"Daddy! Daddy!"

The head did not turn around. The motor of the bus roared.

"Daddy!"

The bus picked up speed.

"Daddy!"

She ran after the bus until she realized it was too far away for her to possibly catch up. Her father was too far away.

Homeward bound, her footsteps were dejected. Her legs felt heavy. Her head felt light. She felt dizzy and lost.

SUNDAY AFTERNOON
July 16, 1961

"I rode a chariot
in a corner of the wind."

Abby tried not to think too hard about her father. She
threw herself into practicing her singing for anniversary
day and remembering her baking lessons.

When anniversary day finally rolled around, five
churches came from across Oklahoma: Missionary Church
of God in Christ from Watonga; St. Paul's from Ardmore;
the Lighthouse Church from Sweetwater; Bishop Green's
church from Boley—an all-black town; and Evergreen
Church from Stillwater.

"Good afternoon," Abby greeted all the guests she passed
on her way to church. As the people began to filter into Solid
Rock behind Abby, they nodded their approval at her neat
appearance. Her blue dress rustled with every step she took. It
had been starched stiff and ironed until its blue cloth shone

almost with a satin hue. The white lace on the sleeves accented the creation. Her mother had French-braided her hair into six plaits, three parallel rows on each side of the part extending from the center of the forehead to the nape of her neck.

"God bless the child," Mother Barker said when she saw how pretty Abby looked.

Solid Rock Church was company clean. Its floors and pews had been dusted and swept. The panes, sparkling from vinegar wash, allowed the stained-glass windows of Jesus and the angels to make miracles with light; a purple robe appeared on the benches, an angel's wings in the aisles.

Everyone knew Abyssinia was one of the best singers in the state, even if she was only ten years old. It was her honor to begin the services with her favorite hymn, "I'll Fly Away." In her patent leather shoes, she tapped out the notes to the opening hymn, shy and quick, her honeyed voice fluttered over the church fans.

I'll fly away, O glory,
I'll fly away.
When I die,
Hallelujah, by and by
I'll fly away!

Mother Barker sat with her eyes closed, her flower-decorated white hat teetering on her head. Abby's sweet song carried her past the pain in her leg, past the brittleness of old age.

Suddenly it seemed as though a streak of lightning scratched across the sky, and the old woman was on her feet. Stretching herself out, she did a holy dance inside the rhythm. One hand behind her back, the other waving at something in the air. And then just as suddenly, she fell over into a faint, her flower garden strewn brilliant on the floor.

"I'll fly away, O glory . . ."

The church continued the song. Patience fanned Mother Barker.

Abby sat back down with the congregation. The song continued.

Abby sat transfixed, the song going all inside her to the very edges of her nerves and clinging there. The music settled in behind her eyes where it threatened to spill out down her face, the way beautiful music sometimes did.

"When I die, hallelujah, by and by . . ."

The melody reached the rafters, and Abby's mother joined the dance, stretching out a circle. Every time she tried to sit down, the organ moaned and screamed louder. The song reached out and held her, then let her go, then gathered her up again.

"Yes, yes, yes . . ."

The congregation sang the words long. Each "yes" meant something different, something deep and wonderful to each voice.

To Abyssinia, it seemed like a mighty wind tore through the place and shook the church members like leaves. People began falling into the aisles and running, running. Sometimes in one place, sometimes up and down the bench rows. Some folks still sat quietly humming with their arms wrapped around their waists, afraid they might lose themselves.

"We had us a service today!" a sister from Ardmore said afterward as they spilled out of the church.

"Amen," the minister from Watonga agreed.

"Abyssinia rocked the church house," said a mother from Sweetwater.

"Yes, Lord," commented Mother Barker.

Already the women had begun to spread the embroidery-clothed tables with slabs of barbecue, pots of collard greens, pans of cornbread, platters of chocolate cake, bowls of black-eyed peas, plates of fried chicken, dippers of homemade ice cream, and Abyssinia's pound cake.

Of all the cakes displayed, Abyssinia's was the first to go. Folks swore it tasted "as good as Mother Barker's." Just in the nick of time, Abyssinia remembered her promise to Brother Jacobs. She reached and wrapped up the last piece of cake in a napkin.

*"This road is a wound
on the hard rock of my journey."*

"Mama, can I take these buckets to the Jacobses'?" Abyssinia asked.

Patience sat on the porch, shelling peas. She said, "Yeah, but you bring your hips back here before the lightning bugs come out."

"Yes, ma'am." Abyssinia placed the piece of cake she had saved in one of the buckets.

When she started down the road, Lily stopped her.

"Abyssinia, can I go?" she asked.

"No, Lily. I'll be right back. Just going to old Brother Jacobs' to return his pails."

The truth was she relished being by herself. Alone, she had time to watch daisies and the crested blue jays and to contemplate the shadows made by the sun on the church house walls.

She had to pass the shack where Trembling Sally stayed. After the tornado, the townsmen got together and began to build a house for the unfortunate woman. They never got a chance to finish the building. The wonderful house they had quickly hammered nails into and sawed planks for out of the goodness of their hearts would remain just a shack. Trembling Sally always ran them away.

A feeling of terror struck Abby as she approached the path that led by the shack. Suddenly she saw the woman rummaging in her neighbor's garbage can. She wore layers of clothing that got in her way as she tried to push the leftover food she found into the shopping bag she always carried.

Trembling Sally looked up and saw Abby. The woman's eyes burned coals of fire. A frown frightened the corners of her mouth; a scowl stormed her face. She muttered rough words that Abby could not understand. She shook her fists menacingly at the young girl.

Abby hurried on her way to the fading sound of the curses falling from Trembling Sally's lips, and she wondered why the woman hated her so. Trembling Sally did make a menace of herself with the other children, frightening them from their paths when she walked the streets, but she especially detested Abyssinia.

Abyssinia wondered why. Perhaps Trembling Sally remembered that Abyssinia was one of the first people she had seen after the tornado. Perhaps she remembered that Abyssinia had taken her to Mother Barker who had no cure or answer for Sally's affliction. Perhaps she thought Abby knew some lifesaving riddle: maybe the way out of this puzzle was a mystery, a secret that the innocent girl willingly withheld from the trembling woman.

Abby tried to recapture the peace she had anticipated during her walk, but it was gone. In its place she felt a vague foreboding. Her stomach cramped. Her eyes began to water for no apparent reason. Soon she could see the Jacobs residence.

"Over here, Abby." The voice came out at her unexpectedly. The pails roughly scraped her legs as she swung around. She walked into the yard and followed the voice.

"Where are you, Brother Jacobs?"

"Over here." The voice came from the barn where the cows were. She headed that way.

He wore overalls and a straw hat. She said, "Brought your buckets back, Brother Jacobs, and some cake like you asked me to."

"Thank you," he said, but he did not look at the cake, nor did he invite her into the house so Sister Jacobs could offer her some fresh-baked cookies and ice-cold lemonade.

"Rest yourself a while," he said. He patted a space beside him on a bale of hay, which she promptly sank into. She snuggled her toes in the dry blades of hay.

"How's Sister Jacobs?" she asked.

"She's visiting her folks in Ardmore," he answered. His voice had taken on a roughness, like the feel of sandpaper under a soft hand.

He looked down at her tiny feet and noticed that the hands rubbing them were just as small.

A wind rustled the hay.

He called her name, "Abby."

When she looked up, she did not recognize him because his eyes were not the same. All she could remember was something someone had told her about the eyes being the windows of the soul. What was wrong with his windows, she wondered.

He gripped her by the toes as she moved to run. In her terror all she could remember was the expression "eyes are the windows of the soul, eyes are the windows of the soul." Brother Jacobs was a friend, a deacon in the church. What had happened to his soul that he should cover her mouth so she could not cry out?

He forced her into the hay and on her back, and then unbuttoned his overalls. He came toward her. She was too scared to scream.

She fainted several times.

Soon she heard thunder, but there was no storm. She saw a pansy wither, but there was only hay surrounding her. She heard the raw cry of birds and felt the sky rain down mud.

Suddenly the sun went out and called lightning bugs forth. On their wings flew death, fluorescent and green. Death touched her body, changed his mind, and flew away.

Patience began to worry when Abyssinia did not come home by the time the lightning bugs were out. She went looking for her.

She saw the girl's feet first, then the dried blood. She screamed. Then said over and over to herself, "Oh, my Lord. Oh, my baby. Oh, my Lord. Oh, my child."

She stooped down and pulled her daughter's dress below her knees.

Patience's legs were weak, but a permeating strength welled up in her from some deep source. She picked up her child. Patience carried her through the night, a fragile fluff of life.

Mother Barker saw them coming down the road.

"Trouble," she said, approaching the mother and daughter.

"Abyssinia," was all Patience answered.

Mother Barker walked the rest of the way home with them. She spoke softly to the unconscious child in Patience's arms.

"You are a marmalade of joy. Precious as the honey inside fallen apricots. Dear as the glow from rubbed gold."

The doctor came. He gave the child a shot and left medication for her. Abby slept for two days. When she finally awakened, the women gentled her.

Mother Barker's sedative hands touched through and beyond the dimensions of Abby's flesh, but it was not enough.

The women left the bedroom and went to the living room.

Mother Barker and Patience spoke to each other in hushed voices.

"It is not the physical wound I worry about," said Mother Barker.

"Salt and time will heal that," agreed Patience.

"The right amount with water," nodded Mother Barker.

"And the crisp petals of a purple bloom. Death and life in its blossom," commented Patience. "Dark decay on its fringes," she commented, "and bright birth in its center."

"No, it's not the physical hurt that bothers me. I look in her eyes, and I see blood on the flower of her spirit," said Mother Barker.

"It calls for other means," said Patience.

"Other medicine. Other balm," responded Mother Barker.

"All injuries need time."

"All injuries need medicines peculiar to the hurt."

"We must apply the balm."

"And then wait for the healing to finish."

The two women knew how looks could heal. They extracted honey from their distilled glances.

Every day one of them would take up the sentry of mercy, would stand gazing down with abundant compassion and assurance at the bewildered child.

When looking, each woman imagined a miracle. Mother Barker imagined the flower ceremonies of spring. Patience imagined the sparkle in a bird's throat. Mother Barker saw a fierce, abiding affection tempered by the fire flickering from the sacred shrine of her heart. Patience meditated on energy from the indelible spirit stored beneath the rich colors of her skin and hair.

It was a time for healing. A double ritual. A duet of waiting.

One afternoon while staring at the child, a song danced from between Patience's lips. Mother Barker joined her, humming an unchained melody:

Restore to the child
Her mirror of enchantment
A hymn of beauty
In the sacred music
Of head and heart rhyming.

They gave her a cup of boiled, steaming water, a secret ingredient added. They gave her water, for water is holy.

They decided to attend Abyssinia seven more days.

Each day one of the women would collect the sun in the pools of her eyes, then go stare at the child. One day mother. One day godmother.

They soothed her with a shower of healing glances, a brush of eyelashes on the bruise of her mind. With a touch as gentle as cotton swabs.

Finally the child dreamed that they took her flying to the home of the wind, opened his gate, and she swallowed the turquoise blue of the sky.

The women smiled and waited.

Wednesday Afternoon
July 19, 1961

"Whoever heard of anybody having pneumonia in the summertime?" Abby's Aunt Serena said worriedly to her sister Sadonia who shook her head in despair. They watched Mother Barker leaning on her cane, slowly walking toward Abby's house. In her free hand Mother Barker carried her basket of medicinal herbs.

Nobody knew where she found her supply of leaves. Folks said she did her field marketing way out in the country somewhere. Where else could an old woman like Mother Barker get tapin's blood for the youngsters to drink when they had whooping cough?

For Abby's pneumonia, Mother Barker took brown spiderwebs, rolled them up in a ball, and made the child swallow them. Mother Barker covered the child with pomachristian leaves and pulled the white sheet up to her chin until the fever came out and set the leaves on fire.

Friday afternoon Serena and Sadonia remarked on the fact that Abby's pneumonia was gone and it must have been the terrible thing that had happened to her that made her susceptible to pneumonia in the summertime. And wasn't it awful that Strong had gone away.

While Serena and Sadonia and the rest of the town went about its business, Trembling Sally sneaked into Abyssinia's room when no one was looking. Her eyes glared hatefully at the disabled child.

"Ain't nothing wrong with you," she accused, standing there trembling and shaking at the foot of Abby's bed. "You just got the people fooled. Can't talk, huh? Can't read, huh? Can't write, huh? You ain't got me fooled. You think you're smart." Trembling Sally shook her trembling finger at Abby.

"How come you can't read now? Aw yeah, you smart all right. You think you have the answers for everything and everybody. All those lessons you used to write for the teacher, where is your pretty penmanship now? Huh?"

The sick woman moved to the side of Abby's bed and breathed her rank breath into her face.

"You're so smart, what you doing letting Brother

Jacobs do what he did to you? You're sly, that's all. Got the people fooled."

Trembling Sally moved a little closer and peered into Abby's eyes.

"But you haven't got me fooled. What you need is some kind of punishment. They got you laying up in the bed, treating you like you're sick. Give me a chance, I'll straighten you out. Give me two minutes alone with you, I'll fix you. We'll see just how sick you really are."

Abby's eyes followed the deranged woman around the room as Trembling Sally moved away from her. Abby remembered her mother was close, down the street at a quilting bee. She knew Patience would soon be in to bring her a warm bowl of rice, some toast, and a pot of tea.

Trembling Sally stood at the end of the bed, her eyes coals of fire. Her layers of clothes hung from her body haphazardly like the shabby wardrobe of a scarecrow.

"Wish I had a stick. I'd fix your red wagon, laying down there thinking you're so smart."

Abby looked over toward the window to see if her mother was coming. She spotted a wasp. It circled the room, buzzing against the curtains, trying to get out. Sweat popped out on Abby's upper lip when the wasp suddenly zoomed toward the bed. Her breath came in short spurts.

"Where's your nightingale voice now, Abby? Can't

sing? Sing for me, little one. Sing now in that sweet voice. Cat got your tongue?"

The wasp hovered.

"Sing, Abby, sing."

Trembling Sally saw the wasp. "You scared of the wasp, Abby?" It was more a statement than a question.

The wasp flew low, its legs hanging down heavily as it flew across the bed again. Suddenly the wasp turned and flew to the window once more. They watched the wasp draw up its legs and hum away through the opening in the curtain and into the honeysuckle outside the window. Then Trembling Sally turned and was also gone.

Abby had passed her days in bed, watching old movies and television soaps: *As the World Turns* and *Search for Tomorrow.*

Cherokee Strip Day arrived. On Cherokee Strip Day there was an annual parade in the name of the Iroquoian Indians who were relocated from North Carolina and Georgia to Oklahoma. The parade generally lasted for hours and was one event that no one in Ponca liked to miss.

"I wish you could come, Abby," Patience said, bringing a cup of tea brewed from chamomile flowers, raspberry leaves, hawthorn berries, and skullcap to Abby's bedside.

Abby smiled, but she did not speak. To Patience's dismay, Abby still was not speaking.

"I won't be gone long," Patience promised.

On Grand Avenue the Cherokee Indians beat drums and marched proudly, their heads adorned with feathers and beads. The fringes of their costumes wiggled in rhythm to their movements as their red faces led the parade down the clay-dusted street. Girls in Shirley Temple curls spun batons with artificial flowers swirling from the ends, their spiffy boots snapping in time to the trombones and cymbals. The marching councils of men came next, flashing flags and fraternal smiles.

A moving float with a blond queen and her attendants inexplicably sent shivers down Patience's spine, even though it was a warm summer evening. More floats passed, but she could not shake the dark foreboding. She began to run, disrupting the steps of the marching band whose path she crossed. Fear whipped at her heels as she ran down the empty streets toward home.

Abby had napped. In her dream she saw a woman dressed for December, in gloves, high boots, and a long-sleeved shirt with a wool cap pulled down over her face. She was carrying something on the shovel she used to clean away the snow from the path in winter. She had a net over her face.

"Mama! Mama! Mama!"

"Abby!" Patience called as she ran past the almost deaf

Mother Barker, past Attucks schoolhouse, past Solid Rock Church of God in Christ.

Patience heard the screams a block away. When she reached the house, Patience tore the screen door off its hinges and flew into the living room, upsetting the chairs standing neatly in the path of the bedroom. She flung the door open on Abby and the sound of wasps. Hundreds of wasps, wasps crawling on the bed, wasps on the pillow. Wasps in her Abby's braids.

"Lightning and thunder follow me around.
Where are my bridges?"

Serena, Sadonia, and Sister Lightsey pondered as they sat on the spinster sisters' porch, watching Mother Barker cane her way down the street to Abyssinia's house. They wondered how the wasps got into Abby's room this Cherokee Strip Day and gave her back her tongue.

"Couldn't any wasp nests have been in that house," said Serena, "clean as Patience is."

"Maybe they got in through the window," Sadonia said.

"I reckon so," Sister Lightsey agreed. "Isn't that something, the child is talking again!"

"It is strange," said Sadonia.

"'The Lord works in strange ways His wonders to perform,'" Serena quoted the Bible.

"Yeah, but there's some of the Lord's creatures I'd just as soon not tangle with," Sister Lightsey announced. "Wasps is one of them."

Over at Abby's house, Mother Barker had set up a corner of the room to apply her folk medicine to Abby's body.

"The lightning bugs are out tonight, Mother Barker," Abyssinia said.

"Now that's the truth, honey," the old woman agreed as she applied snuff spit to the stings on Abby's face.

"Mother Barker, there's something about lightning bugs," Abby said.

"What, daughter?"

"How come they shine like that?"

"They've got a light in their belly."

"But how come lightning bugs are here?"

"You mean down here on the earth?"

"Yes, ma'am."

"For the same reason we're here, daughter. He put them here.

Mother Barker pasted the snuff spit between Abby's braids. "Maybe they were sent to give children something to play with in the evening time. A lightning bug is nothing but one of God's toys for children."

It seemed to Abby that it had been raining forever. The streets were swollen with rain. From her bed she listened to the steady fall of rain as she read Shakespeare, the poetry of the Book of Psalms, and the plays of Langston Hughes.

This night the Oklahoma River rose. The creeks left their crevices and spilled out onto the surrounding land. The Lightseys, who lived on land lower than Abby's family, barely had time to get out before the floodwaters covered their property. They cooped up their chickens and put them on the roof. Old man Lightsey loaded down the Ford with their valuables—bags of flour, sugar, cornmeal, grits, dried onions, potatoes, and rice. The rest of the family heaped the children's red wagons with quilts and clothing.

Young Bill Lightsey pulled a milk cow on a long rope, her metal bell clanging and resounding all over town.

Through her bedroom window, Abby looked down the hill and watched the Lightseys and the other lowland residents crawl up the hill like crawdads crawling up a riverbank. Behind them the river waters had quickly inched up the buildings they had left behind so that now she could only see the rooftops of chicken coops. The rushing water covered the tree trunks, and the treetops looked like shrubbery floating in a pond.

That night twenty people bedded down at Abby's house. Her young friends flitted in and out of her bedroom. At first they whispered when they spoke to her, then they forgot themselves and talked in louder voices. Soon they were shrieking and laughing. She joined them in their giggling and their games of Simon Says.

"Simon says, 'Roll your eyes,'" Lily Norene said.

Abby rolled her eyes from side to side, the black in them shining like polished obsidian.

"Simon says, 'Touch your nose.'" Abby's small hand reached up and touched her plump nose.

"Simon says, 'Stick out your lips!'" Abby pushed her generous lips out even farther.

When sleep overwhelmed them, the children and the adults spread pallets all over the house. The smaller

Lightsey children slept by the foot of Abby's bed. Brother and Sister Lightsey spent the night on the living room floor, while the older children slumbered on the kitchen linoleum.

The next day Abby could smell from her sick bed the delicious vapors from the pots of mustard greens the women had prepared and sat on the stove to simmer. At supper they served her cornbread and the greens with cha-cha—the pickle relish of hot peppers, green tomatoes, cabbage, and spices that the women had canned last autumn.

She spooned the cha-cha onto her greens. Bill Lightsey had milked the cow the morning before the flood and had made fresh butter from the cream. She spread the butter thickly over the hot, golden cornbread.

Once again that evening, the children gathered around Abby's bedside to continue their game of Simon Says.

"Touch your ears," Lily Norene said.

Abby giggled. She would not get caught touching her ears when Simon had not told her to.

"Simon says, 'Take two steps forward.'" All the children took their first steps forward. Somewhere between the first and second step, they realized that Abyssinia would not be able to comply.

"Aw, shucks!" Lily said, embarrassed by her error.

Abyssinia pulled the bedcovers aside and stuck out her foot. She eased the other one down alongside it and finally stood on wobbly legs. Bill Lightsey rushed toward her to help, but she motioned him back. She took one unsteady step forward. The children let out one long, collective sigh.

Unsteadily Abyssinia managed her second step.

The children let out a victory scream and began clapping loudly. Patience rushed into the room to see what all the commotion was about.

"Lord, have mercy!" she said upon seeing Abby standing.

Before the floodwaters receded, Abby was up out of her bed and stirring around, just as she used to do.

One day the Lightseys waved their good-byes as they repacked their quilts and supplies to go back and clean up the black silt the Oklahoma River had left on their floors, windowsills, and walls. They went back to let their chickens loose to scatter themselves in the yard and to let the cow roam unroped in the field.

Sister Lightsey asked, "Daughter, will I see you in church Sunday?"

"Yes, ma'am. I'll be there." Abby smiled, now up and standing on the porch, watching the children and Sister

Lightsey begin to pull their loaded wagons back down the hill.

But when Abyssinia got to church that Sunday, she did not sing. And neither did she utter a word about the wasps.

On the way home from church, Lily asked her, "What was it like, Abby?"

Abby knew by the way Lily emphasized "it" that she was talking about what Brother Jacobs had done.

She looked around to see who could be listening. There was no one within hearing range.

Abby's throat tightened as she opened her mouth to explain. "I felt dirty. Dirtier than playing in the mud. The kind of dirt you can't ever wash off. . . ." She could not continue.

Lily Norene allowed her the hesitation. She did not say anything. She did not want to rush her.

"It hurt," Abby continued.

"Real bad?"

Abby nodded her head yes. She found her voice again. "But the worst part was I felt like I was being spit on by God."

"Girl!"

"Like I must have done something mean and sinful. Something so wrong. Something so wicked." She stopped walking. "I must have tempted Brother Jacobs."

"No, you didn't. The devil got into Brother Jacobs. God wouldn't allow . . ."

"How do you know?" Abby screamed. "It didn't happen to you!"

"I know God wouldn't . . ."

"You don't know anything!" Abby screamed at her friend. "God knew about it!" Abby said this last part so loud and painfully that Lily did not know what to say.

Abyssinia started running toward home by herself.

"Wait up, Abby," Lily called, but Abby would not answer. Abby would not look back. She ran home as fast as she could.

That day Abyssinia gave God's gift back to Him. They had told her that her singing was a "gift from God."

She did not trust any of His gifts, she thought. She did not want His gifts for she could not tolerate His punishments. She did not want His presence in her life for the absence of His grace was awful.

She passed two of the church deacons on her flight home.

One of them said, "I don't know how Brother Jacobs could hurt that innocent child."

"And his wife took it hard."

"Took Sister Jacobs a long time to choose a husband."

"See how he do her."

"She look for the sun, she find shade."

"A bone-chilling shade. Near about killed her when she found out, the shock."

"Sat on the porch in that rocking chair, rocking for a month, her mouth clamped together like clams."

"Hear her moan with every creak of the rocker."

"Wasn't she at the child's birth? Loved Abyssinia like the children she never had."

The men stared silently after the retreating Abby. Finally one of them added, "I hear Jacobs turned himself in."

"If I had Patience looking for me, don't you know I'd give myself up, too!"

"Brother, I agree. I'd rather turn myself in to the law than have that woman mad at me. She's too nice. Some people take niceness for weakness, but I know better. Nice people can be as merciless as they can be kind. And that's a fact."

WEDNESDAY AFTERNOON
December 5, 1962

Although Brother Jacobs was gone and Abby's speaking voice had returned, the Jackson world was not secure. The money saved from their cotton field labor was all used up, and the Better Way Barbershop income was no longer forthcoming. A family could ordinarily glean a living without handouts from the county, but these were not ordinary times for the Jackson household.

Abby's teacher, Miss Pat, sympathetically called the county after several months had passed and Strong had not returned to support his family.

Abby remembered the day the county woman came. Patience had gone to visit Sister Lightsey, and Abby entertained herself by cutting out paper dolls from old newspapers.

The county woman knocked at the door.

Abyssinia peered at her through the crack in the door. The woman in the gray wool coat and galoshes with the rock-blue eyes and automatic smile did not look anything like Jane's mother in the reading books at school. The woman's cheeks were not rosy and pink, like Jane's mother's cheeks, but were pale and pasty, like dough that needs kneading.

That's what Mother Barker meant, Abby thought, when she said, "Their bread's not quite brown."

Abby opened the door.

"Is this the Jackson household?"

"Yes, ma'am."

"Is Mrs. Jackson at home?"

"No, ma'am."

"Well, I'm from the county."

"Ma'am?"

"Miss Miller, from the county," she repeated impatiently.

"My mama's not home."

"Yes, you told me. I'll wait for her." The woman entered the house without being invited.

Once inside, the county woman looked Abby up and down like she was inspecting a can of vegetables on a store shelf.

"You must be Abyssinia."

"Yes, ma'am."

Miss Miller did not sit on the couch to wait. She roamed through the front room, her eyes darting here and there. Her inquisitive fingers lifted the cover off the empty candy dish. She picked up a little glass squirrel from the whatnot shelf, peered at it, and then sat it back down. She examined the lace doily on the back of the couch. She went into the kitchen and peered under the cabinet, looking for rats and roaches. She ran her fingers over the freshly washed dishes.

Abby's heart thumped maddeningly in her breast, a razor rage growing along the edges of her young nerves.

When the county woman came back to the girl standing in the living room, shifting her weight from foot to foot, she hiked up the girl's dress to inspect the cleanliness of her drawers. Abby shrieked and ran out of the room. She came back brandishing a sour mop still wet from that afternoon's scrubbing.

"Get out of here, you white witch!" she yelled.

The county woman retreated a step. "I won't authorize you to get one cent from this county if you don't put that thing down, you dirty nigger!"

Abby flew into a rage. She thrust the dirty mop into the woman's face. The woman turned purple and ran, screeching, out of the house. As she flew down the steps,

Abby bopped her on the back of the head with the mop handle.

After the county woman roared off in her county Ford, Abby returned the mop to its proper place. She picked up her paper dolls and wondered how somebody so white could treat people so dirty.

*"My song tamed fire; with my voice
I waded water."*

This fall they feasted on wild greens. Patience had it all fig-
ured out, a different variety of greens for each day of the week.

"I'm fixing some poke salad greens today," she told Abby.

Then the next day it was speckled dick, and yet another
evening she fixed lamb quarters mixed with wild mustard
and wild turnips.

"I'm fixing gr—" she started to say one day but
changed it to, "I'm fixing my plate."

Before long they were tasting the juice from the poke
salad that had gone to seed, from which they had made
pokeberry wine. Patience allowed Abby to drink a small
glassful for "medicinal purposes."

They continued to sup from the canning and created
meals from the backyard garden of tomatoes, string beans,

okra, corn, and fruit that came from the trees.

Patience promised the landlord that she would make up the rent past due "when cotton-picking season comes," and the landlord, knowing her to be a woman of her word, let them stay on in the house.

When Patience heard Brother Jacobs was getting out of the penitentiary, she asked the Lord to give her strength. Opening the Bible randomly, she read Psalms 129:1, "Sorely have they afflicted me from my youth, yet they have not prevailed against me."

Patience interpreted that Biblical verse as a sign that she would triumph over the evil Brother Jacobs had wrought. The town said she was a fanatic, spending her days on her knees, praying.

Then one day Patience got up off her knees and climbed up in the loft and brought down Strong's double-barreled shotgun. She polished its gray metal with a piece of flannel until it gleamed cold silver. She parked the long gun next to her Bible on a table by her front window. She kept the window shining clean and the curtain pulled back so that all her astonished porch-sitting neighbors could see.

Evidently word reached Brother Jacobs before he could come that way from the penitentiary. The rumor was that he never even stopped in Ponca City but headed for parts unknown on a Southern Pacific train.

WEDNESDAY NIGHT

August 19, 1964

Abby was attracted to the social gatherings that always
seemed to accompany the white cotton harvest in August.
It was where all the most interesting playmates her age
could be found. The Lightseys with their army of thirteen
children and the Macon family of a dozen boys numbered
among the cotton field chosen ones.

The cotton was high, the voices were cheerful, and
although the work was hard, it was not without its rewards.
The learning of new songs, mostly spirituals, was one
source of cotton field entertainment.

Another was the stories the old women told on their
porches, stories that could scare the daylights out of any
man, woman, or child. The storytellers spoke with easy
familiarity, as if they held daily conversations with haints

and ghosts. They said that the warm and cold spots a person might feel while walking in the middle of the road represented certain spirits come back from the dead.

In the daytime, in the light of the sun, these tales were not discomforting. But in the evening, the haunting tales sent chills down a listener's spine.

"Tell the one about the man searching for his head," Sister Lightsey said to Mother Barker.

"No, I want to hear about the woman looking for her children in the graveyard," someone else begged.

"Let's listen to Abby tonight," Mother Barker decided.

Abyssinia had become so adept at retelling the stories she had heard season after season that the old folks made way for her to tell a tale every now and then.

Abby waited until the lightning bugs flitted green around their heads and the moon had gone to silver, casting a strange, grayish white lunar light on the cotton patches, which grew right up to the cabin door. An eerie feeling like spiderwebs would creep over the listeners when Abyssinia began to speak, her voice shivering. The people gathered, and the older children whispered to the younger ones to be quiet, their thin "Ssshes" floating like shadows on the night air.

"Once there was a little girl named Lubelle who liked to play with snakes," Abby began.

To her listeners, a snake was one of the most frightening and fascinating creatures that ever crawled on the earth; in fact, anything that crawled was suspected of being an instrument of the devil.

"That ole snake, Satan," one porch-sitter responded.

"And this Lubelle, she kept her room dirty, dirty," Abby continued.

"Cleanliness is next to godliness," Sister Lightsey admonished.

"It was so dirty that Lubelle had trouble finding her bed at night."

"Lawd!"

"It would take her near 'bout two hours to plow from the bedroom door to where she slept."

"Talking 'bout dirty!"

"Why, her windows were so dingy and dirty even the sun couldn't get in."

"Help, mercy!"

"In her room it was always night."

"Tell it!"

"But there wasn't no stars."

"Hmph!"

"Her ceiling was black, and if you tried to light a lamp, you might burn down the whole house."

"What you say?"

"Lubelle had clothes strewn from the ceiling to the cellar. When she woke up in the morning, the way she decided what to wear was whatever she wrapped her hand around when she opened her eyes, that was her costume."

"Well!"

"She even took her food in the room and went into the closet where she fed the snake."

"Hush."

"When the snake first came into the closet, he was a little bitty thing, no bigger than a worm."

"Child!"

"But as the dirty girl fed it, it got bigger and rounder and longer." Abby stretched out her arms and made the snake grow.

"It got so it would wriggle its way to the mouth of the closet and wait for Lubelle to appear. And she always would."

"Jesus!"

"Then one day her mama got sick and tired of telling her about the mess in her room."

"Sho' nuff."

"She got tired of saying, 'Honey, clean up your room.' 'Child, get this 'bomination together.' 'Daughter, God don't like ugly, ugly peoples, or ugly 'pearances.' And she grabbed the child and stepped off into the dark 'pearance of the room."

"Well!"

"And she began to throw clothes out of the room this-a-way and that-a-way."

"Help, mercy!"

"She worked her way on over to where the window would be, then sent the child for a bucket of water and apple cider vinegar, and made her scrub the glass.

"Listen here!"

"And she scrubbed off legions of dirt."

"Legions!"

"Armies of dirt marched into her rag and into the bucket of vinegar water 'til the bucket was filled with mud."

"Dirty, Lord, dirty!"

"Then pretty soon through the window you could see the outline of the sun."

"Daylight!"

"You could see daylight a-creeping through the win-dowpane."

"Hmph!"

"And as she worked, the sun came a little closer."

"Closer!"

"Then she could feel the warmth of the sun as it started to beam on into the room."

"Lit up the room, child!"

"And on the last rinse of cider vinegar water, the sun came streaming through, lighting up the place like a candle in a dark cave."

"Hallelujah!"

"But what the light showed there, y'all would be astonished—the child's room had cobwebs thick as grandma's lace. She had a pile of bones over in the corner. You woulda thought you had stumbled upon a burial mound. Her layin'-down bed looked like a sow's sty and smelled far worse."

"Whew!"

"And the mama commenced to throwing out bones, knocking down cobwebs, and took the slick black sheet off the bed and sent it out to be burned."

"Help, mercy!"

"Finally they made their way on over to the closet. And Lubelle commenced to hollering, 'No, Mama, don't go in yonder.'"

"What you say?"

"'Course the mama plowed her way on into the closet and began chucking out stuff 'til she came upon that ol' snake, Satan."

"Lord, Lord!"

"And she let out a scream song so long and loud even the croaking frogs down by the levee quieted. She said,

'Father, have mercy. Spare us today, Lord. My child is living in this den of dirt and iniquity, and please don't let the snake bite!'"

"Hold him, Lord!"

"And the daughter, she hollered for a different reason."

"Uh-hum!"

"Because she loved the snake. But the mama, she went and fetched her cotton-chopping hoe and said, 'Daughter, move!'

"And the daughter, she screamed and hollered for the mama to spare the snake."

"Ain't the devil something?"

"But the mama took aim at that long, low devil."

"Well?"

"And she chopped the devil's head off his wicked neck."

"Tell it!"

"And the snake snook no more."

"No more, Lord!"

"But that ain't the end of our story."

The people were now rocking to the rhythm of Abyssinia's tale.

"And they buried the snake, and the child took sick."

"Took low."

"The mama hung fresh muslin curtains in her room, and still she pined."

"Pined!"

"Changed her bed to boiled sheets and lye-soaped her floors and walls."

"Yes, ma'am!"

"And still she grew weaker."

"Help, mercy!"

"I say, they made her dolls and set them in her closet door."

"Tell it!"

"And then her legs refused to walk. They brought persimmon wine and peppergrass greens, and still she was failing."

"Hmph!"

And on the night of the full moon, her skin turned dry, and they gave her water."

"Help, mercy!"

"But before the dawn . . ."

The audience was on its feet now.

"But before the dawn . . ."

The cotton pickers begged her to finish.

"Before the dawn, she dried up, and her skin peeled from her body like the scales from a black poison snake."

"Do, Jesus!"

Abby let her voice drop two inches. "And after they wrapped her in her winding sheet, they buried her in a watery grave next to the coal-black snake. And today, in the spot where they both rest, you will find a black-berry vine. They say she is the berries, and the snake is the stickers.

"And if you want to get a Lubelle berry . . .

"I say if you want to eat a berry . . .

"If you want to taste a Lubelle berry, you got to go through the snake."

At the lunch breaks during the harvesting of the cotton, Abby used to play ring games with Lily Norene and the Lightsey children. They would weave in and out of each other's arms, chanting:

Draw a bucket of water
For my lady's daughter
One berry bush, two berry bush
Three berry bush
And pretty little girl creeps under . . .

They chanted in a child's breath sweet as apples and gave off the perfumed, musky smell of young sweat into the early evening air.

Plant my cotton in the middle of May.
If I don't make cotton, I do make hay.
Ever since my dog been dead,
Hog been rotting my potato bed.
Give my cow rotten ear corn,
Give my cow holler horn.

But this cotton-picking season, Abby and her friends stopped playing for no reason that Abby could discern. They now moved uneasily with mingled embarrassment and pride. They stood on the sidelines and watched their younger brothers and sisters go through the childhood rituals:

Plant my cotton in the middle of May.
If I don't make cotton, I do make hay . . .

The older folks knew that something new had developed in the blood and souls of these youngsters who were neither children nor grown-ups.

Abby found herself listening more faithfully to the songs of the elders. She especially liked the image of movement in the lyrics—"painting pictures with words," she called it.

Her mind was flooded with questions and wonderings.

How often had she heard "The Gospel Train"? Did it have a new meaning for her now that she was older? Would she ever sing again? Would she ever recapture that quality in her voice the church members had admired so when she was younger? How did she feel about God's gift now? How could she deny her Father in heaven if she truly longed for her father on earth? Four years Strong had been gone. Four years she had longed for his return. Was he somewhere laughing? Laughing without her and Patience, or was he sad and lonely, starving and thirsty for their abiding devotion?

Perhaps even now he was returning to them, maybe he was riding on a train, a train bringing him back to them.

Next to Abby, Sister Lightsey opened her mouth wide and unashamedly twisted her lips this way and that, screwing up her face like she was tasting pickles. Abby remembered that Sister Lightsey always said, "You can't look beautiful when you sing. Haven't you noticed how the best singers look downright ugly when they open their mouths in song?"

The gospel train is coming,
I hear it just at hand.
I hear the car wheels moving
And rumbling through the land

Get on board, little children
Get on board, little children
Get on board, little children
For there's room for many a more . . .

The elders joined Sister Lightsey on the chorus, a sure sign that her song was heartfelt.

The fare is cheap and all can go,
The rich and poor are there.
No second-class on board the train,
No difference in the fare . . .

Then the entire choir of cotton field singers chimed in.

Get on board, little children
Get on board, little children
Get on board, little children
For there's room for many a more.

"Lord, Lord!" Sister Lightsey said after the singing was through. It was one of those days when everybody was of one accord.

On the way back to the cabin, the air hung like heavy curtains around Abby. It was so hot she felt like she was
standing next to the oven on baking day. Where her eyes
spied open earth, the clay seemed scorched. Where the
earth was carpeted, the grass grew green from the sudden
summer rainstorms that came and went so abruptly. This
hot evening the sky was smudged with red. The searing
sun was a red stove eye in the Oklahoma sky.

Abyssinia felt singed by the sun's flame. She thought
about the Chickaskin River's wet invitation. A cool bap-
tism for her parched skin.

She stepped into the Chickaskin to relieve herself
from the hot judgment of the sun. She swam back and
forth across the meandering stream. After a while she

rested and stood up in the most shallow part, her sundress sticking to her body.

She thought she saw the shadow of a person moving between the cottonwood trees that bent over the mirror of the water. She wiped away the moisture drops trickling down her face. What was it she saw?

She shook her head and blinked water from her eyes. She saw only a flock of shrikes flying playfully from tree to tree.

In the distance she heard the lonesome call of the Southern Pacific train. Trains, planes, and buses reminded her of her father. When is he coming back? she wondered.

She ducked her head under the water and held her breath a few seconds. Surfacing, she stroked a few more feet out into the creek.

Agilely turning on her back, she kicked her feet rhythmically and paddled farther out. After she plunged beneath the cool current, she blew sweet bubbles to the surface, breaking the calm of the unworried water. She treaded water until she was cooled from the relentless heat.

She leisurely stroked her way back to where she had stepped into the river.

When she looked up, she saw Trembling Sally step up to the edge of the water, close enough to touch her.

Abby wanted to flee, but the water impeded her

movement. She was not swift enough. She splashed away from the riverbank, but had only gone a few feet when Trembling Sally was upon her.

"I knew I'd get you! I knew it!"

The woman was a warped log thick in the waves. Her powerful arms seemed to blot out the sun and were unhampered by her bulky apparel. The deranged woman's layers of clothing floated on the water like the tormented petals from some strange flower.

She grabbed Abby by the shoulders and held her under the vise of her grip.

Silently Abby prayed, *God who made music, hear me.*

Abby could smell the foul, stinking breath of the older woman. She felt the mighty hands push her under.

Abby held her breath and fought back. She struggled free, gulping the fresh air.

The mad woman hurled her under the current again. Abby fought back harder. It was not enough.

God, who has dominion over ritual sound, hear me.

The woman plowed the girl's head into the river. From somewhere Abby found the strength to surface again. Trembling Sally caught her hands in the ropes of Abby's hair and pulled her down again.

God, who can hear the cry in a voice and rinse it 'til it is crystal and honey, hear me.

It was harder now. Abby did not know if she would ever break free. She was sure she would die in the river. She swallowed water. The world began to spin. She heard the ocean roaring in her head.

God, if you let me live, one day I shall sing all the words in my song all the days of my life.

Then she could hear the crazy woman laughing from far off. A crazy, wild, shrill, triumphant laugh. The water pounded the girl until she was ground down to nothing.

Finally she could smell the eternity of the sea.

The water rippled no more.

She knew certain things. She knew Trembling Sally was gone and that she was out of the wet danger and lying on the dry ground.

For a long time someone had been pressing the river from her lungs. Her head felt swollen with throbbing pain. Her lungs burned, waterlogged, and her limbs trembled, heavy and grotesque. She struggled to breathe. She felt let down and lifted up. She felt lost and saved. She tried to blink, but the strong sun locked her eyes closed.

"You're going to live, Abby. I promise you that."

She thought she heard her father's voice. Of course, it was not her father. Her father had deserted her and had left her to be shamed by Brother Jacobs and drowned by Trembling Sally.

She thought she could hear her own heart dying. She was drifting away. A gray fog enveloped her spirit. Her very soul sagged.

"You can do it!" she heard from afar. "That's my Abby. That's my baby!"

Was she saved from everlasting hell? Was she to be reborn? Her father's hands were a warm bandage. Her father's voice was a healing balm.

She opened her eyes and smelled the familiar breath of her father. "I'm here, Abby. I'll never leave you."

He breathed for her. Then she was breathing with him. Then she was breathing for herself. She had found her father. She had found her father again.

Strong had ridden the train back home. A bus bore him away, but it was the clacking sounds of the railroad tracks that haunted him home. What kind, benevolent force had led him past the creek on his way to Patience's cabin in the cotton field? What force had guided him there just then?

Abby watched Strong working daily in the field, and in the evening he chopped wood for the fireplace and spent the dark evenings gazing into the mystery of the flames—no flame was ever the same. Soon she knew he would rebuild his barbershop. But it would not be the same. Just as each flame that flickered changed, he had changed. Life would be different. A kaleidoscope of ever changing patterns.

Often Abby found Strong and Patience seated side by side, gazing into the magic of the fire, and something inside her began to mend into a seamless scar. She wanted the healing to be so complete that soon no one could tell where the cut had been made on her soul. The skin of the scar would fade into a thin line; she would be bound with hope, faith, and renewed wonder.

---

*"In my private garden flows a fountain
of sparkling water. Come drink, you won't
ever be thirsty again."*

Late this afternoon on a Ponca City porch, Abby sat with the women and discussed the day's events. Sister Lightsey had dragged Trembling Sally out of some fire ashes in the morning, and later on Trembling Sally had tried to poison the Lightsey children for laughing at her. She went into their hiding places and cajoled them to her shack where she tried to serve them oleander tea. Mother Barker just happened to drop by for a visit and rescued them.

"I know it was rosebay," Mother Barker said.

"Rosebay!?" said the astonished Abby. "Why, that'll kill you!"

"How could you tell it was rosebay?" someone asked.

"By the way it smelled," said Mother Barker.

"Oleander does have a peculiar smell all right," one of the women agreed.

"Then I saw the petals," Mother Barker revealed. "The children kept arguing over who had the most blossoms floating in their teacups."

"Poor little innocents," the snuff dipper said.

"What can be done about her?" asked Abby.

"She might really harm somebody someday," the snuff dipper said.

"She bears close watching," Mother Barker said quietly to the concerned woman.

"You know, even after I got them away from there, the children still wanted those purple blossoms. Said they were pretty. Children will be children."

"Wonder if she's through fooling with Abby?"

"Hard to tell. The woman has a scar on her. Left by the tornado. Imagine she thinks Abby's the cause."

"I didn't do anything," responded Abby.

"We know, daughter," said Mother Barker sympathetically.

"She's got the spirit of a tornado," the snuff dipper added.

"Who?"

"Trembling Sally."

"What she is is a devastation," someone said.

"Can't tell what she's going to do."

"A tornado must be a woman," Abby decided.

The women on the porch clicked their agreement with their sewing needles.

Mother Barker sighed and sucked her teeth.

That night Abby dreamed that she heard the rustling of strange cloth and an insistent voice whispering that the Tornado and Trembling Sally had become one.

Abby spun around and stared into the red-pepper eyes of the tornado. Now since the tornado was a spirit, she could come through cracks. Wrapped in her web of mystery, she began speaking to the startled Abyssinia in a voice belching with fire.

"Oh, yes," the tornado began, "I am the only storm in the sky. Thunder and lightning comfort me. They duel every winter over who will court me. The truth is I give them both a brief glimpse into my eternal eye. They both like my fire, the way I twist when I walk. The way I move quietly through earth and swish through air and water.

"I've seen you down on your knees complaining about me. How dare you call yourself telling on me! Praying to your God with your mouth all primped like prunes!"

Then the tornado started pacing up and down. Where she walked, sparks flew.

"Yes, I trouble the water. Yes, I walk through flames,

and I eat fire. Yes, I step in harm's way and challenge danger. You think twice. I think once and move on. I blister my feet bronze walking through smoldering ashes. I run mad with the wind.

"You little cautious twerp, how dare you bow your head and scandalize my name. I, too, am a child of God. When He created me, He fashioned immortal art. I am a spirit with nerves of petrified stone. I am the emboldened dark girl of His heart.

"He designed and sewed this gray dress of silk and steel, fit for a tempest. See this red stitching on my sleeve and hem? He did that. My blizzard hair, my whirlwind arms, the stare of my cyclone eye, He patterned.

"I blow the landscape raw. I sneeze and my wings of wind astonish the hurricane. I stub my toe and a typhoon appears.

"My Father gave me power over the currents of the wind. Therefore I come when I please and leave when I choose," she said, running her electric fingers through her hair with a whoosh-whoosh and swishing her gray dress trimmed in fiery red. "Why, I haven't done you nothing yet," she said.

She stopped in front of Abby, "Why, I was just playing. Would you like to see me do some real work?"

"Oh, no," Abby hastened to say, staring into the

tornado's whirlpool eyes. "I can see you are a rare woman. An extraordinary figure. Free!"

Abby approached the tornado spirit. She studied the peerless pattern, the perfect pleats, the silver-crimson color, the careful cut and precious fabric. "Where did He find this material?" Abby wondered, rubbing the exquisite cloth through her fingers.

For an instant Abby stared in silence at the tornado. Then the tornado smiled a rare rainbow smile, ran her fingers through her unkempt hair, and whirled off a piece of her dress the size of a handkerchief. She placed the smoky electric cloth in Abby's surprised hands.

Abby saw the woman turn and step into her bright chariot of smoke and fire.

In her dream Abyssinia watched the mist gather around the tornado's chariot as she stepped inside and tightened her hands on the reins.

She turned around to say, "Abyssinia, makes no difference what damage I done. One thing you must remember is this—I had no choice but to harness the wind!"

SATURDAY EVENING
September 10, 1966

Abby and the other women sat outside under a pair of pecan trees, repairing their cotton sacks and watching Mother Barker cook. They had worked hard in the cotton, Monday through Saturday noon. Now it was Saturday evening, and Mother Barker had been stirring up pans of crackling bread and simmering pinto beans seasoned with fatback for hours in the huge cast-iron kettle. She had baked blackberry cobblers and an Oklahoma pecan cake to celebrate Abby's fifteenth birthday. The cobblers sat cooling on the windowsill. The cake had been ready long before she baked the crackling bread and was displayed on the long table where Abby and the women sat. Missing from the group was Ruby Jean who was in her cabin asleep.

"Maybe Ruby's just missing her husband," someone remarked.

"That's a fine husband for you. Here she is expecting any day now, and he can't be found. Can't see hide nor hair of him."

"Maybe she needs to find herself somebody else," Mother Barker said.

"She's already got a husband," Abby reminded them.

"Sometimes it takes a while to find the right one," Mother Barker emphasized.

"Mother Barker, how many times have you been married?"

"Four to be exact."

"Doesn't the Bible say 'Keep thee only unto one husband'?" Patience quoted.

"If the Bible says that, all right."

"I know you believe in the Bible, mother," Sister Lightsey hummed.

"I do."

"And aren't you saved?"

"I am."

Yes, she's saved, thought Abby. She had personally seen Mother Barker shout.

"I recollect the Bible also says," Mother Barker continued, "'What God has joined together let no man put asunder.' Well, God's been nowhere near some of these ugly-acting wonders!"

She stirred the pot of beans and continued to contemplate. "I reckon what you got to understand is this here."

"What's that, Mother Barker?" Patience asked.

"What you got to understand is that every man you marry is not your husband."

The women discussed this proposal as the light filtered through the leaves of the pecan trees, casting shadows of lace on their faces.

"That man Ruby Jean married might be worrying her, but that baby is worrying me," Mother Barker confided.

"When'd you examine her last?"

"Yesterday morning."

"How'd it look?"

"Not too good."

"Not too good?"

"No, ma'am."

"Well, what's the matter?"

"She carrying it too high in her stomach," Mother Barker announced.

"They say you carry girls high and boys low."

"No," Mother Barker insisted, "this is different. She's carrying this one different."

"I guess you know."

Mother Barker stitched on her quilt, her brows furrowed.

"Baby past due and still setting up in her chest."

The women exchanged glances. Mother Barker generally knew what she was talking about when it came to medicine and babies.

"She never laughs. Not even a smile. Not good to act like that carrying a child. Child might come here . . ." She bit off a thread along with the rest of her sentence.

"What, Mother Barker?"

"Never mind," she answered.

The midwife had watched women give birth to strange-looking babies, some with water on the head and others so deformed that even she had to turn her head to the wall. In these cases, Mother Barker would tell the mother to roll on the baby. When they buried the unfortunate child, word would spread that the midwife had not even let the mother see it, for many a mother took sick and even died upon seeing the monstrosity that had come from her womb.

---

*"I danced through smoldering canyons
overrun with briars, stickers,
and sharp stones."*

It was hard for Abby to believe that she had reached her junior year in school. She stood at the classroom window, tracing patterns on the frosted panes.

A small worry nagged at the back of her mind. She was part of the committee for the annual Christmas program. Every year she had offered some small token of her talent, a poem, a speech, and when she could sing, a song.

Now it was just two weeks before the program.

"This year, my dear students, we're going to have the best Christmas program ever. Everybody knows nobody celebrates Christmas like Attucks," the principal bragged.

Already Abby was forming in her mind the story she would tell. Maybe a ghost story, maybe the Lubelle story.

The principal began assigning to each student a role on the program. When he got to Abby's name, he said, "And Abby, you will render us a song."

"No!" she said, so forcefully that she startled herself. "I mean"—Abby blushed—"may I do something else besides sing?"

"We have you down for singing," the principal reaffirmed. Some of the students who were members of Abby's church nodded as they remembered Abby's earlier electrifying musical performances.

"But I don't sing anymore," she told the principal. Two freshmen—neophytes vain in their recent entrance into high school—snickered.

"Young lady," said the principal, "I expect you to be a shining example for our younger students. We have you down for singing 'The Christmas Song.'"

"But . . ."

"The program is already made up. December thirteenth, that's the date. Eight o'clock, our usual time. Usual place. Phillis Wheatley Auditorium."

"I'd prefer to recite a poem or . . ."

"I know your talent for singing, Abyssinia Jackson, so we even placed you in the featured position at the end of the program."

"Saving the best for last," a senior agreed.

"But I can't," Abby insisted.

"False modesty will get you nowhere," the principal assured her.

"You don't understand, something happened to my voice," she trembled.

"You speak okay. Time to set old things aside. Anyway, there couldn't be too much wrong with your singing. Besides, as I explained to you, the program is already printed."

Monday Afternoon
December 12, 1966

For the past two weeks Abby had worried and worked. She had torn into her books feverishly.

Her exams showed that she excelled in certain subjects. Paul Laurence Dunbar poems were as familiar to her as the "Lord's Prayer." When her literature teacher asked for a comparative analysis of Dunbar and Langston Hughes, she knew she was academically on safe ground. She concentrated on literature, biology, and chemistry classes, while avoiding music classes, the glee club, and the Attucks choral sessions.

Lily Norene, who had done well in her rhetoric classes and her general education courses, had found it hard to understand Abby's feverish pace. Lily waited for her in the hallway.

"Abby!" she called to her.

Abby stopped. She had been walking with her head down, hurrying to her next class.

"Where've you been? Every time I come by the house to see you, they say you're in your room studying."

"Examination time, you know."

"Same time every year. So what's different about this year? We still managed to spend time with each other before."

"It's just harder this year."

"Are you trying to tell me something? Everybody knows you've got it made gradewise. So what's the real problem? Did I do something? Did I say something wrong?"

"No, I'm sorry. It's not you. It's just . . . Oh, I don't know," she answered, exasperated.

"We are going to the Christmas program together, right?" Lily asked.

"Yes, Lily." This was her perfect opportunity to tell her friend she was scared stiff about the program. But she could not tell her. What was there to say, that she didn't want to sing?

Abby perked up then and said, "I got a class. See you tomorrow around seven thirty."

That night Abby could not sleep.

The next evening she put on a red velvet dress she had sewn herself. Everybody said she looked pretty in red.

She and Lily sat in front with the rest of the program participants. The place was packed.

"You look absolutely blue," Lily Norene said.

"I feel cold all over," she answered.

"You're not catching the flu, are you?" Lily touched her forehead. "No, you don't have a fever."

First on the program were the two freshmen. They performed a skit called "Man Hunting," replete with clichés about acting dumb around males and the advantages of "running after him until he catches you."

The student body applauded politely, and the two young women returned to their seats in the front row.

Another student recited "The Night Before Christmas" in Black English.

It was Christmas Eve, y'all,
All through, under and over the house
Wasn't nothin' stirrin', baby,
Not a rat, nor a mouse. . . .

The student body laughed uproariously and gave the young man a standing ovation when he finished.

Next a flutist played "I'm Dreaming of a White

Christmas," endorsed by a round of warm hand-clapping from the audience. Then Abby heard her name. The principal introduced her as "the treat of the evening."

Abby walked steadily enough to the podium. The piano accompanist began skipping her fingers along the keyboard. Abby opened her mouth, but all that came out was silence. The accompanist stopped and started again. On her cue, Abby opened her mouth a second time. Nothing.

The two freshmen began squirming in the front row below her. The pianist started up once more. This time, when Abby opened her mouth, notes came out.

"Chestnuts roasting on an open fire . . ."

But the notes were wrong. Where they should have soared, they sagged. Where they should have sweetly dropped, they screeched.

"Jack Frost nipping at your nose," Abby howled.

The two girls in the front row were laughing so hard they had to wipe their tears away with the backs of their hands.

Finally the accompanist stopped cold. She got up from her seat at the piano and walked off the stage. Abby stumbled after her, embarrassed to death.

---

*"I stayed long at her altar and stared
deep into her sanctified eye."*

"I'm sure glad you stopped by, child. Haven't seen you for a month. Nobody can read the *Black Dispatch* like you can. I had one youngster over here and she read it so fast I couldn't keep up with the news. Like she was in a hurry to get away."

"She just didn't know, Mother Barker," Abby said in her loudest speaking voice.

"Maybe so. I don't know about young folks these days." Mother Barker tapped on her hearing aid. "How's your mama and daddy?"

"They're fine, Mother Barker."

"And your friend, Lily Norene?"

"You know she got married before the end of her senior year, just before she graduated. Never did finish."

"Somebody nice or somebody trifling?"

"The latter."

"What, daughter?"

"I said I don't think he's nice to her."

"Hmph," she said, looking off.

"How's the foreman, Mother Barker?"

"He's doing poorly, daughter. I don't know . . ." A look of sadness crossed her face. Then she changed the subject. "This child that was reading to me showed me your picture in the *Black Dispatch*. Said you got the honors from the school."

"That's right, but that won't help me in Ponca City. There are no medical schools here."

"Then do you think you'll be traveling on, too?"

"I want to go to medical school very much. I've been studying quite a few brochures of colleges that prepare you for entrance."

"Well, when will you be leaving?"

"I don't feel it yet, Mother Barker."

The old woman brightened at Abby's response. "Tell me, what was high school like?"

"Lots of things to study and read."

"Like the *Black Dispatch*?"

"Mostly not."

"What then?"

"Well . . ." Abby's mind raced ahead, trying to find the

right thing. She remembered a poem she had memorized by James Weldon Johnson.

Abby began reciting and talking about God calling the angel on his right.

"Woo! I can see the bright angel now, Abby."

"'And death heard the summons and leaped on his fastest horse, pale as a sheet in the moonlight.'"

"Ride on, death," Mother Barker said.

Mother Barker breathed with the story. She could see Sister Caroline laboring in the vineyard of life. She felt her tiredness, her weariness. Mother Barker's eyes glistened when Abby finished the story.

"Abby, I'm glad you finished high school and got yourself a nice education."

"It wasn't always nice, Mother Barker." Abby told the story of her humiliation at the Christmas program.

Mother Barker looked intensely at Abyssinia, remembering the circumstances of her birth. "Tuck this in your memory, Abby. The music's still there. It's running through your soul like a deep river. Daughter, you're destined to unbearable pain and unspeakable joy. A whole lot of both."

"Why?" Abby wondered.

"Child, when they filled your cup, they put in honey, but they didn't leave out the lemon. You don't know what I'm talking about now, but you will."

The foreman's wife studied the young woman sitting in the rocking chair opposite her.

"Abby," Mother Barker continued, "I have some things I want to tell you."

"Ma'am?"

"You remember the cake recipe I learnt you that summer?"

"Yes, ma'am. Do you want me to bake one for you?"

"No, there's something else I want to show you. But it's gonna take longer than one hour."

"Another recipe, Mother Barker?"

"Lots of them."

"What kind of cake? What pie will you show me how to bake?"

"No cake, no pie."

"Then what?"

Mother Barker was quiet for a minute. Then she said, "My mama and her mama before her knew certain things."

"What things?"

"Powerful things. Things about healing, about birthing, about fixing."

"Fixing? You mean about roots?"

"About working roots, too."

"Mother Barker, do you think . . . do you think I'm supposed to know?"

"You're supposed to know, child."

"How can you tell?"

"Oh, I just know. I've always been knowing." Mother Barker looked out the window, lost in thought. When she spoke, she looked directly into the younger woman's eyes. "You stay with me two months."

"But that's so special. You think I'm special, Mother Barker?"

"It's not for everybody," Mother Barker agreed.

"Why me?"

"I can't be telling you that, daughter. It's rooted in secrecy."

"Mother Barker, you know, some folks call it old fogey talk, superstition."

The old woman did not hear her. "When I get through, you'll be a special doctor. And if somebody tries to do you some evil, sprinkle some seeds of mustard around your door."

"But, Mother Barker, you're so good. Can't some of those practices cause other folks harm?"

"Well, fact is, I haven't always been good. Old age has a way of mellowing the outrages of youth. When I was young, I used to do all kind of stuff to folks out to do me wrong."

"Mother Barker, I can't imagine . . ."

"I threw salt after one woman who was after my

husband. Woman moved so many times from house to house 'til she broke down the moving wagon. Salted her good. One ornery man made me so mad I rotted the teeth out of his head."

Mother Barker chuckled at the memory of her past exploits. And then her voice became more serious.

"Working roots is powerful, daughter. And you have already been crowned. You were born with the veil, and you were born when the sun was high in the sky."

Mother Barker looked up at the sun shining through her living room window.

"These here are mysteries they don't know about in the schools. There's power in you. Why, you could hit a straight lick with a crooked stick if you wanted to. And if you wished it, folks wouldn't want to meet you walking nor riding."

The old woman folded her hands in her lap and set her rocking chair in motion. She nodded her head as she rocked, stressing her agreement with the words she had just spoken.

"Why don't you just tell me the sweet part, where you do good for people?" Abby implored.

"The good part? The sweet part?" Mother Barker thought for a minute. "I got to give you the bitter and the sweet. I can't give you the light without showing you the dark."

Mother Barker and Abby went to the fields where they gathered herbs. In the graveyard they gathered goofer dust, dust from the graves of infants. On the way home from the cemetery, Mother Barker instructed her in the difference between dust from the graves of sinful grown-ups and dust from the graves of innocent babes.

After they had collected bat blood, sarsaparilla root, and pomegranate hulls, Mother Barker said, "Daughter, it won't be long before these educated doctors will be running out of medicine."

"Running out, Mother?"

"The medicines will stop working because they're moving away from Mother Nature. All kinds of people will be coming to you the minute I'm gone and they find out you know. Especially the menfolk. They're so low-lifed, some of them. They catch all kinds of diseases. When one comes at you with the running range . . ."

"The running range?"

"Some of these young tappins lately have been calling it the claps, but it's the running range. When they come to you with the running range, you get yourself some blackberry roots, a pinch of alum, put them together in a pot, and start it to boiling. When it gets to boiling, stick in a pinch of soap and nine drops of turpentine. Tell him to take the quart of medicine home and drink it for water. Make it last nine days. Running range won't run again, I promise you."

"Mother Barker, how'd you come to know all of this?"

"It's rooted in secrecy, daughter. I'll give you the history later. Now the young men will come to you with the running range," she added. "The old ones will come to you with the rheumatism. For the rheumatism, you go get some mullen leaves. No more than seven, and steep them in a quart of water. Then you tell the man to drink at least four half-glasses a day. Tell him he ought to make the quart last him for two days."

The next day, Mother Barker and Abyssinia were visited by a man with bladder trouble and another with lockjaw. A woman needed a remedy for being sick at the stomach. A child was in need of a tonic.

After three weeks Abby got her first patient. A woman, doubled over with cramps, came to the door. She was bleeding so profusely from her period that she was flooding. Mother Barker inspected the insides of the woman's eyelids.

"Inside of her lids looks like white turnips," Mother Barker diagnosed. "You know what to do, daughter."

Abby fetched a whole nutmeg and grated it into a quart of water. Pouring the water into a kettle, she added a pinch of alum. She boiled the potion for three minutes.

Later, after the tea had steeped, the old healer and the young apprentice watched the ailing woman go on her way with her jar of medicine. Abby folded her arms across her chest, proud that she had brought relief to somebody in pain.

Mother Barker quietly interpreted the pleasure and awe in Abby's face, and then said, "Promise me this, Abby. You will make this a Healing House when I'm gone."

"A Healing House?"

"For the body and the soul."

"You're not going anywhere," said Abby.

"I shall go where we all must when my time here is over."

"But how can you speak of it?" Abby wondered aloud already feeling a sense of loss.

"I already talked it over with Barker. He's in agreement. The house will be yours."

Mother Barker registered the look of hurt and bewilderment in the young woman's eyes.

"You're the only child we have, Abby. Even if Patience did give you birth and Strong is your daddy."

Mother Barker stacked a smaller pot into a larger one and added, "I know this house is not much to look at." This was an understatement. The house was a great deal to look at.

In one room Abby and Mother Barker had catalogued roots. They had placed herbs in boxes and jars. Dried leaves hung down from the ceiling. Abby had studied the plants, their long, slender roots, the rivers of veins and fire that ran through the leaves, the dance of colors on the dried petals. She knew them by heart. Outside in the fall the garden was a miracle in green. Now in the kitchen they continued to sterilize the healing pots and jars until they gleamed.

"You are an arrow in the bow of a benevolent wind."

"What?" asked Abby, now listening intently.

"My child, there is no greater joy on earth than the joy of healing."

That night Abby dreamed of a soft, peaceful place where healing sights and healing sounds dwelled. She stood under a rushing waterfall. Showers of stars cascaded about her. Silver chimes tinkled in the darkness; the wind whispered secrets. Suddenly an enchanted candle lit the night, and she saw rainbows laced through canyons, birds flitting through the branches of trees towering on the face of the moon. She heard faraway strings plucked on a guitar at dawn.

Then her dream turned. She heard a girl child singing: "Feed my soul and water well this spirit . . ."

The child's voice lifted fine and high, like a bell at dawn. It seemed to come up through layers of light, light veils. The sound drifted through a distant drumming, through a flurry of flutes, through the soft, sparrowed notes of an unseen harp. The girl child's voice floated through a river of soprano vibration. The last veil, a circle of echoes whispering memory within memory, slowly lifted, and Abyssinia woke up.

TUESDAY MORNING
November 7, 1967

The squeak of Mother Barker's rocking chair was a soothing rhythm that she and her ailing husband only faintly heard. He lay very still in the bed next to the rocker where she sat, unaware of the rain falling in heavy drops drumming against the windowpane.

Entering their bedroom, Abby balanced the tray with the pot of broom wheat tea and the two matching porcelain cups so the spoons would not clink against the china. She set the tray on the nightstand between the bed and the rocker.

"Thank you, daughter."

"You're welcome." She retreated to a place by the window and watched Mother Barker pick up one of the cups, stand next to the bed, and spoon-feed the foreman. He slurped the tea thirstily. Abby smiled to herself at the picture of two old people loving their lives out. So that's what "in sickness and in health" means, she said to herself. Then the sound of water splashing against the pane behind her caught her attention, and she turned to watch the water form evanescent patterns on the glass. Little rivers and valleys ran and vanished into other streams and crystal creations.

She heard Mother Barker ask her husband, "Barker, you want some more tea?"

"No, baby, that's enough."

Abby turned away from the window and faced them, studying the image of the old people.

Mother Barker set the cup on its tray and rearranged the nine-patch quilt on his frail frame. She ran her hands across his brow and suddenly tensed.

"Barker, you all right?" she asked.

"I'm glad you're here, baby," he answered.

She reached in the nightstand and got his comb and parted his thick white hair. She gently scratched the flakes of dandruff from his scalp.

"You're a comfort," he managed to whisper. "Mama, it's been a good life."

"Oh, it has, Barker."

"You ever been sorry about us?"

"No, Barker, I've been mighty glad. You, Barker?"

"Me? I've been satisfied since I first looked into your doe eyes. Remember the day you waited for me under the mulberry bush. You fluttered your dark eyes flecked with pride at me. Pretty." He was quiet again, remembering. "My daddy told me the blacker the berry, the sweeter the juice. Now I know what he meant. I been blessed ever since I saw you picking cotton that first time. When you stood up at the end of your row, I could see you had country legs. A blackberry-colored, dark-eyed, bowlegged woman."

A thin smile lit Mother Barker's face like a candle. She made another part in his hair and continued the soothing scratching of his scalp and combing of his hair.

"Barker," she said so softly Abby had to strain her ears to hear, "you're the only husband I ever knew."

"Is that right, baby?" he asked, gladness making his old voice lilt youthfully.

"That's the truth, Barker. You were my sweet song in the morning, my candle in the midnight. You, sir, were my everything." They both laughed together. She stooped over and pecked him on the cheek. Her trembling hand parted his hair again.

For a few moments the only sound Abby could hear was the rainwater sloshing against the pane. Then she heard the rough sound of Barker's labored breathing. A spasm racked his body. He caught his breath and shuddered.

"What's it feel like, Daddy?" Mother Barker asked.

He did not answer her at first. Then he sighed. "Like barbed wire in my side."

Mother Barker sucked in her breath and tightened her trembling hand on the soft, wooly texture of his hair. She made another part in his scalp.

"I want to be released, Mama," he said.

"Released, Barker?"

"Released from these hooks, from this barbed wire hooking me in the side."

Mother Barker gasped. A fat tear fell from her eye into the sick man's parted scalp.

"Is that oil you're putting on my scalp, baby?"

"The moistest kind, Barker."

"Feels good," he said.

"Lord, Barker, death will only part us for no longer than it takes to harvest one season." She put the comb back in the drawer. "You hear the rain outside on the windowpane, Barker?"

He turned his head toward Abby and the window. They had forgotten she was there. Mother Barker turned up her hearing aid so she could listen more intently to the rain.

"You know when the snow falls, you can't hear a thing," Mother Barker said.

"That's the truth, baby."

"In the next life we will work other miracles, Barker. I bound you, we will hear the snow."

The old man cackled softly. Mother Barker moved her rocking chair closer to his bed and sat down. They held hands in the still solitude of the day.

Abyssinia tiptoed out of the room.

Abby dressed in black wool for Mother Barker's funeral. A veil of fine lace from the dead woman's closet covered her face.

The deceased had predicted the month and year of her death. She had told Abby the summer before, the summer her husband the foreman had gone on to glory, "On the eve of snow, I'm going to die. Death will come riding, will come riding on the third cloud of the storm. God'll be sending an extra light in the night, and it won't be the moon."

The Oklahoma River heaved on the night Mother Barker died. The river waves licked the air above them and fell back convulsively upon themselves. The night Mother Barker died, a string of stars fell from the sky; it contained pearls of lightning.

Sister Lightsey told Patience that Mother Barker had requested that Abby sing "Deep River" at the funeral.

"Are you sure?" Abby asked when Patience told her.

Then she remembered what Mother Barker had said about the Christmas program at Attucks. "Daughter, the music's still there. It's running through your soul like a deep river."

On the day of the funeral, folks packed the church house even to the rafters. The touch of Mother Barker's hand had extended for generations; she had helped and healed many. They came to say good-bye to the healer and to appraise her apprentice, Abby—or Abyssinia, as they began to call her.

The minister was reading a scripture from the Book of Psalms. Abby sat in deep thought. Before she knew it the minister was requesting that "Abyssinia Jackson come up here and sing 'Deep River' for the passing over of Mother Barker."

Could she? She was rooted to her seat, paralyzed.

Could she? Patience, sitting next to her, gently pushed her, answering the unspoken question.

Abby stood up, but she could not move. Her mind said, "Move!" but her body would not obey. An usher reached for her hand. Strong said, "Go on, daughter."

Somehow Abyssinia got from her seat to the aisle. She

could feel the trapped melodies pushing against her heart. She could hear the lost notes trembling, trembling on the borders of her soul. The song was waiting to be let loose, waiting to be set free, waiting for the chambers of her heart to open so the music could ring out ripe and full.

The song began creeping from the deep recesses of her soul, and her body began spinning in the aisle. In a series of small, spinning circles, she stitched her steps to the front altar.

While the church held its breath, her voice wove its way from within the cavities of her heart. A sweet, sweet sound poured from her mouth. The notes hung silver above the congregation.

> *Deep river, my home is over Jordan*
> *Deep river, Lord,*
> *I want to cross over into campground . . .*

Abyssinia stretched out her hand, and the organ joined her.

"Lord, I want to cross over into campground . . ."

Her feet stepped over into campground, and she was suddenly before Mother Barker's casket. Her hand reached over and touched the folded hands of the woman in the white, satin-lined coffin.

Abyssinia sang the last verse.

Oh, don't you want to go to that gospel feast,
That promised land where all is peace?
Lord, I want to cross over into campground,
Lord, I want to cross over into campground.

It was an extraordinary passing. At the cemetery they lowered Mother Barker's body into the ground.

"Dust to dust," the minister said.

When the body was safely, snugly covered with dirt, the town went its way.

The space Mother Barker left was immense. A spirit had passed, and the townsfolk mourned. The people went to bed lamenting that Mother Barker was gone but reminding themselves that Abyssinia was there.

During the night a deep frosting of snow covered the town. Dawn sifted itself over the world, and a stark coldness whispered over the land.

Drawing back the curtain from her bedroom window, Abby looked over at Mother Barker's empty house. She saw them perched on her late mentor's roof. She saw them—a circle of snowbirds.

Letting go of the curtain, she smiled to herself. Mother Barker was right.

*"Seven petals of honeysuckle I crushed,
then bathed away the purple pain."*

Lily Norene Johnson's house sat back off the road, surrounded by an unpainted wooden fence. Old cars and trucks littered the yard. Patches of red dirt peeked up through the snow. A string of icicles hung from the roof.

It was one of the few house calls Abyssinia had made. Usually the patients came to her. But it was difficult for her old friend Lily to leave her home, so Abyssinia had put on her wool coat and rubber boots and trudged through the snow.

When Lily answered the door, Abyssinia gasped; her face was a mask of welts, bruises, and darkened circles. Her left hand was twisted, and she carried it limply before her. Her right hand held a baby in diapers. Another tot, just learning to walk, tugged at the hem of her cotton skirt. Lily's hair stood out in disarray over her head. Her shoulders were stooped, and in her eyes fear crouched.

It was common knowledge that Willie Johnson beat his wife, Lily Norene. Sometimes he was more vicious than usual, and on those occasions she was left with another missing tooth, another scar, or some permanent disability like the twisted hand. The beatings also left her with more responsibility than she had before. In her five years of marriage to the man, she bore him five children.

Abyssinia took off her coat and went to the kitchen where she sat a pan of water on the stove. She asked Lily what happened.

"He beat me." Lily spoke in a soft, suppressed voice.

"You know, there are ways to stop him from beating you."

After the water began boiling, Abby took a pouch out of her dress pocket and sprinkled oil of lavender and crushed Japanese honeysuckle into the water. She let the mixture steep.

"Call the police, they look at you like you're some kind of old dog," Lily said.

"Have you tried that?"

"No. Winnie Mae told me about the time she tried

talking to the law. They think you must like getting whipped."

Abyssinia took a piece of red flannel out of another pocket and soaked it in the steeped mixture.

"Maybe that's because nobody ever beat them," she told Lily.

"Women don't ever beat men," said Lily Norene.

"Now and then you hear of a case. A little scrawny woman attacking a big, husky man.

"Come on in the living room and lay across the couch," Abby said. Lily laid the baby beside her on the sagging sofa. Abyssinia carried the pan into the living room. She took a cloth and dipped it in the mixture, then soothingly bathed Lily's bruised face. "I want you to go see a doctor about that hand and a dentist about your teeth."

"Where will I get the money?"

"Do something. Get county help if you can't take in some washing or ironing. You can't let this go on. Your body can't stand . . ."

"What?"

"Never mind. Is he jealous?"

"Of what? There's nobody else. With all these babies, I don't have time to even comb my hair."

"Are you jealous of him?"

"Maybe I am," Lily said haltingly.

The baby beside Lily on the couch began to cry. The toddler tugged at her skirt. The other three children, all girls, sat in a corner, silent and afraid. The baby cried louder. His noisy squalling was a wall between the two adults and the children.

"What about your girls? You've got to do something. Else they'll think that's what women are for—beating."

Lily looked at the older children and shook her head; tears flowed like an unchecked river along the black and blue landscape of her face. The infant squalled louder and flailed his arms.

"With him hollering, they can't hear what I'm saying," Lily said, referring to the older children, "so I can talk plain."

Abyssinia creased her brow in a look of concern as she contemplated the three girls huddled in the corner. "Why do you stay?" Abby wondered.

Lily said, "I guess I love him even though he strays. I believe he loves me. Sometimes I look at him and the love is so deep that my knees get weak. And Abby, sometimes he's so gentle. I tell you I've seen him pick up stray dogs and feed them. He can be tender. . . . Once when my head was hurting, he brought me a bouquet of flowers just so he could see me smile."

The baby's screams had intensified. His face was red with anger.

Lily spoke again. "Now if you can stop him from beating me without meddling in the rest of his gentle ways, you're all right."

Abyssinia was perplexed. She could not advise throwing salt after him since that would make him go away all together.

"I'm leaving you some extra medicine. Lily, dress your hand every day and bathe your face with the remaining brew. I'll stop back by another time."

*"I am but a cinder in the snow.
Who could gaze at me long
and deny I passed through fire?"*

On this winter afternoon Abyssinia carried a pot of vegetable stew from Lily Norene's stove to the table. She looked outside and called the three girls in from their winter game of hide-and-seek. The two younger children were staying with their grandparents, Lily Norene's mother and father.

"Yoo-hoo, come to supper."

In an Oklahoma winter, evening fell suddenly across the white, frosty plain. The sun was there and then it was gone.

The three girls sat around the table, listening to Abyssinia recite a cabin tale so vivid that they saw weasels, foxes, and bears walk across the kitchen floor. They laughed when she did Paul Laurence Dunbar's "At the Party." They obeyed when she said, "Get your elbows off the table." They listened acutely when she divulged beauty secrets for the face: olive oil and lemon juice.

When the dinner was finished, she helped the girls get started on washing the dishes; then she went to the bedroom where Lily lay resting to see if she felt like eating.

"Yes, I think I'd like some preserves to go with the bread," she answered in a whisper so as not to wake the baby lying next to her.

"I'll bring it to you," Abby said as Lily Norene started to move to get up.

"No, I need the exercise. I feel like it," she said pulling on her robe. "I'll go down to the basement and get some."

Abby noticed as Lily walked past her that her hand was almost completely healed.

Abby suddenly shivered as she heard a hoot owl screech in the cold evening. "Lily, don't get chilled," she called.

Lily walked down to the cellar. The cellar was getting dark, but Lily knew that the peach jars would be next to the okra, which was above the shelf with the tomatoes and corn . . . but the row of shiny jars was not there. Only one jar remained. She picked it up.

"What? What happened to the rest of them? They were right here!" she said aloud to herself. "How could they have just disappeared into thin air? What could have happened?"

Then she remembered him sneaking down here, prowling around the jars. "Last year it was the apricots. I should have known. Neglecting his own children to run away to that hussy in Lawton. How dare that man come down here stealing my canning for that lazy heifer?"

The tomato and corn jars began spinning and whirling on the shelf. A pain cracked through her skull like lightning. She dropped the jar of peaches. The carefully sliced pink fruit was speckled with grime from the floor while the peach liquid oozed into the dirt and glass. She vomited on top of the mess.

It took Lily an eternity to get back up the cellar steps. The gummy sound of her feet sticking to the peach preserve syrup she had wasted on the cellar floor haunted her on. She held on to the railing, dragging her body up, up. Her mind pulled down, down one side of her face, leaving it paralyzed. At the top of the steps, she talked out of only one corner of her mouth.

Abyssinia screamed, "Oh, children! Help me with your mama!" She was a little woman, weighing only a hundred pounds. Abby and the children moved her to her bed.

For days Lily Norene lay across the nine-patch-quilted bed. The words only half left her mouth.

"Chiildreeen, doooon't ruuun sooo faast. Ooopen the dooor foooor Abyyy." The sudden stroke had left her speech affected, her body paralyzed. Abby came to clean and cook as often as she could, but nothing helped.

On the winter morning of the final insult, Lily's mind told the right side of her face to fall, too, and when it did, she went out of the reach of pain forever.

Tuesday Night
February 2, 1971

The Ponca City men were remodeling the dining room in Lily Norene's parents' house into two bedrooms in order to accommodate the motherless children. Abby had promised to stay in Lily Norene's house with the three girls for the two weeks it would take the men to finish the building project.

After telling bedtime stories to the girls and kissing them good night, she went to the living room where she unfolded a pair of sheets and some quilts and made a sleeping place on the sofa.

"Hoot, hoot," she heard as she snuggled down between the covers.

Abby wondered about the persistent owl that had been hooting outside Lily's door every night since her death.

When the owl's cries almost wrapped themselves around her, she left the couch to see if she could catch a glimpse of this constant night caller.

The muted light of the crescent moon sprinkled little sparkles of light on the snow. For as far as her eye could see, silver beams brushed the whiteness with sequins. The new snow lay like vanilla frosting over the caked earth. Now snowflakes drifted down through the cold, dark night soundlessly. She thought she heard the quick-quick sound of the greyhound's feet on the road after the rabbit in syncopation with the hoot-hoot of the owl.

"Quick-quick."

"Hoot-hoot."

"Quick."

"Hoot."

She turned the porch light on and saw a flurried, furtive movement away from the light. She knew hungry dogs must eat, yet she hoped the rabbit would get away. She would hate to be a rabbit chased across the chilly maze of the earth with the hooting cries of a night owl at her back.

Suddenly the night grew darker. A cloud curled itself gray in the sky and obscured the moon.

She turned out the porch light and stretched out on the couch with her quilt and fell asleep.

She dreamed she had the feet of a rabbit, and when she ran, her tongue hung from her mouth like the panting tongue of a greyhound. She ran into a meadow sparking with fire that blocked her path. As she circled the meadow, the owl flew through the flames. The dogs howled a hungry call, and the fire barked its response.

She dreamed of flaming wings and the cough of fire.

She dreamed of cries in the night and the helpless whimpering of children.

She dreamed of her old adversary, Trembling Sally, the nuisance who stalked her slumber. Trembling Sally was a troubling woman in the rapids of her dreams, a drunken tempest raging in her inner ear, one who wailed an awful wailing. Her sound scalded peace.

Out of the veil of sleep stepped Mother Barker who whispered, "Abyssinia."

Then louder, "Abyssinia."

Then she screamed strong enough to mend the minds of the demented, "Abyssinia!"

Abyssinia awoke, sat up on the couch, and sniffed.

"Fire!" she screamed.

And Trembling Sally held fire in her trembling hand. She moved catlike and she flashed a Cheshire cat smile at Abby. A mad tigress dancing with fire, Sally opened her mouth and roared red torches.

Abby remembered the sleeping children. She dashed away from the hoarse, rasping woman and into the bedroom, banging the door shut behind her. She pushed a chest of drawers in front of the door to secure it.

"Get up," she shook the wide-eyed children. "Quiet now," she cautioned.

She crumpled the bedcovers over the heads of the startled children to keep out the smoke crawling under the doorway.

"On your hands and knees now. Over by the window. Keep your heads down." They followed her orders obediently.

The raw cry of Trembling Sally cut like a sharp knife through the house as the maniac woman scurried from place to place, torching the furniture and curtains.

Abby had trouble raising the bedroom window. Any moment Trembling Sally would be there with her torch to light up the bedroom, too.

The girls rubbed sleep from their eyes and started crying. Abby signaled to them to be still and quiet, reminding them to keep their heads low and under the rising smoke.

She called upon every power she knew. Straining every muscle in her body into one mighty thrust, she heaved the window open.

The first child scrambled out. They could hear the

chest of drawers Abby had jammed against the bedroom door groaning. Then Abby helped the second child out of the window. When she reached down for the youngest child, Trembling Sally burst through the door, a gust of smoke billowing in with her.

The wild woman let out another tortured wail and, wielding her flaming torch, rushed toward the fleeing Abby.

Abby placed one leg out the window and, clutching the youngest child to her chest, jumped free of Trembling Sally's grasp.

The crazy, hollowed eyes of the woman stared at the free Abby. Then her torch lit the bedroom curtains. Fire danced on the bed, burning the crazy patch quilt, the feather mattress, and the feather pillows. But the fire was not satisfied.

Now the wicked fire demanded more. Its violent, ruby mouth kissed Sally. Sparks leaped up her clothes and sizzled.

The crimson flame licked at the pitiful woman, turning her hair to black straw. Abby sucked in her breath and shuddered. She guided the children's heads away from the horror.

In the distance they heard the disappointed barking of the dogs returning home without their rabbit.

Snow-bearded planks and ice crystals fell between blankets of fire. Snapping, sizzling, frying, the fire dazzled the snow, and the ice bit into the flame with chattering teeth.

By the next afternoon, Abby had taken Lily Norene's three daughters and made them feel welcome in Mother Barker's house, for their rooms at their grandparents' home were still not finished.

Abyssinia sat by the window in what was once Mother Barker's favorite armchair, embroidering a quilt patch of birds. Her quick fingers darted the needle threaded with orange and pink silk strands in and out of a pattern of wings. She paused to rub her eyes and laid the patchwork aside. She picked up a porcelain teapot from the end table and poured the steaming liquid carefully into her cup. She sipped the hot sassafras tea and savored the sound of a tree limb scraping against the window beside her.

The tree was a skeleton of its former self. Its dress of

green leaves had withered, and it had ceased to bear pecans. White snow stuck to the naked, scratching branches. Beyond the trees she could see Lily Norene Johnson's girls, looking like cinders in the snow, running carefully along the treacherous, ice-slick ground. The motherless orphans stopped near the mailbox and began to build a snowman. They packed three mounds of cold snow into balls—a small one for the head and two larger balls for the body— and ripped off a twig from a blackjack tree for the nose. The youngest child produced two pieces of red clay from her pocket for the eyes.

Abby smiled at the snowman's red eyes and stood up to get a better glimpse of the children's creation. She pulled on her boots and overcoat and went out to join them. Digging into the pocket of her coat, she extracted three pennies and handed them to the young Johnsons. The youngsters dressed the snowman in copper buttons. All four of them stood admiring the shiny snowman.

Abby gathered the children around her and showed them how to make snowballs as hard as marbles. The youngsters stooped over the fresh snow and sculpted missiles as big as their fists. Squeals of delight fluttered from their mouths as they ducked each other's snowballs and ran through the cold, crisp Oklahoma air and into the house. Abby followed them inside.

Soon the Ponca City women began to arrive. They came to join Abby in the celebration of the saving of the children's lives. They brought offerings of canned mulberries, okra, collard greens, smoked turkey, and hot pans of yeast rolls recently popped from the oven. They sat in a quilting bee circle stitching bedcovers for the orphans and listening to Abby tell how they had fled the fire and trudged through the snow to the safety and welcome of this residence that had belonged to the Barkers and which was now Abby's home.

"You know," Abby was saying as she served warm pomegranate wine to the women, "when we got here, I scrubbed us all raw. I washed the ashes and smut from our hair and bodies. I rinsed the smoke from the burning eyes of the children. But I could not wash the wailing of that woman from my mind."

The women nodded their heads in silent affirmation of Abby's pain.

In the next hushed moment, they heard Lily's child singing to herself as all children do.

I am but an arrow.
The wind is my bow.
And where I go,
Merciful breezes flow.

Patience, her hair salt and pepper, gray and black, looked at her grown-up daughter and said, "Mother Barker would have been pleased to know you brought the children here."

"To this safe harbor. Yes, Lord," the woman embroidering golden poppies against a background of cotton green squares said.

"We'll prepare them warm rooms of patience. Like we did for Abby," another seamstress added.

"Doesn't matter which house they stay in. Their grandparents will let them stop by from time to time," someone else mentioned.

"They'll always be welcome to visit me," Abby agreed. Suddenly Abby's eyes lit up with understanding. She said, "One day even these girls . . . a continuing circle!"

"Push on, daughter," said Abby's mother Patience, weaving a tomorrow from thread and cloth.

"We'll teach them stories and how to bake bread that rises."

"Have mercy," another answered.

"There are two things children must remember," Patience advised.

"What is that?" asked Abby.

"Fire is warmth, and fire can burn."

"And when it burns . . . ?"

"Yes?" the women echoed in a chorus.

"The holy water of women can mock the fires of hell," Patience witnessed.

"Turn its groaning rages to singing embers," another whispered.

"My, my, my, my, my," the snuff dipper murmured, rocking herself in the rocking chair and unraveling a new spool of thread.

Abby understood, her hands quiet on her cloth.

The women bent their heads and hummed as they sewed in the manner of creative women since back when cotton became thread, then became cloth. But what they hummed was the melody of Lily Norene's child, this melody taught to her by Abby, this melody whose lyrics were a paraphrase from Mother Barker.

Abby bowed her head over the last wing in her quilt patch of birds. For brightness she selected a thread of startling scarlet. For endurance she borrowed the delicate strength of silk. Then she worked the stitches with nimble and quick fingers. She darted the thread with careful precision through the wonderful wings.

Her pattern completed, she looked carefully around the circle of women and, raising her hand in silent gesture, commanded this miracle: "You women of women, you women of mercy, balancing crystals of water on your wings, rise from deep ashes, rise from old ashes, rise etched and marked from scarifications, rise and fly."

In the circle the women saw, and yet did not see. Abyssinia sighed within the inscrutable chambers of her soul, shook dew from her wings, and started the climb.

Reading Group Discussion Guide

1. Describe the setting, background, and era of this novel.

2. At the beginning of several chapters in the novel, you will find short poetic quotes (sometimes called "epigrams"). Choose one epigram from the book and explain how it addresses the principal character in that particular chapter.

3. What is the significance of the name Abyssinia? How might it apply to the main character of this novel?

4. Lily Norene is Abby's best friend. Why do you think they are drawn to each other? How are Lily and Abby different? How are you different from and similar to your best friend?

5. What is a matriarch? Who is the matriarch in *Marked by Fire*, and what makes her such? Who is the matriarch in your life?

6. Compare the role of Mother Barker at the beginning of the book when Abby is born with Abby's role toward the end of the book after Mother Barker dies.

7. What is a nemesis? Who is Abby's nemesis, and what makes her such?

8. What is (are) Abby's special gift(s)? Do you have a special gift? Name one or two special gifts shared by you, your close friends, or your family members.

9. Describe and compare the tragedies that occur in the lives of both Strong and Trembling Sally after the tornado.

10. Discuss why Strong chooses to leave his family after the tornado. What does this say about his love for his family? How is he different when he returns? Describe a similar event that has happened in your life, or in the life of someone close to you.

11. When *Marked by Fire* was published in 1982, the book was banned from some libraries because it contained the word "rape." Why is the word now allowed in the novels available to you today? What has changed since 1982?

12. At what point in the novel do we realize that Abby has lost her faith in God? How do her feelings about her special gift change? Have you ever doubted your own special gift? Explain why and how you were able to reconnect with it.

13. When Abby is asked to sing at the annual Christmas program, her singing voice fails her, and her notes go all wrong: "Where they should have soared, they sagged." What event sparks the miracle of Abby reclaiming her singing voice? Who sets this plan in motion, and why does she do so?

14. After finishing the book, what do you think the title *Marked by Fire* means?

JOYCE CAROL THOMAS'S
Favorite Reads for Teens

I Know Why the Caged Bird Sings by Maya Angelou is a brilliant autobiography chronicling the author's upbringing by her Arkansas grandmother, who supports her through tragedy to her success as a courageous and independent leader of women.

Another inspiring autobiography is *Anne Frank: The Diary of a Young Girl.* What muster it must have taken for Anne Frank to write this book while she was in hiding for two years. Published long after the war ended, this is the story of her people's suffering at the brutal hands of the Nazis during World War II.

The Outsiders by S.E. Hinton is a classic that portrays class differences of yesterday and today through the innocent eyes of boys.

In *Spunk: The Selected Short Stories of Zora Neale Hurston,* you'll find color-rich tales chock-full of tragedy and humor. The book stars the African American working class in the Gulf States.

The Bluest Eye by Toni Morrison—a magical classic. The author unflinchingly illuminates the continuing color conflict challenging dark-skinned African American girls.

The Fountainhead by Ayn Rand tells the enthralling story of young architect Howard Roark, who breaks with tradition by ignoring his adversaries and following his unique artistic vision, thereby leaving the world his legacy of landmark icons.

I've also found *Ceremony* by Leslie Silko to be a great read. Her book recounts the heroic story of a half-white Laguna Indian ravaged by World War II, who finds his personal peace through spiritual healing.

The Joy Luck Club by Amy Tan powerfully portrays the lives of two generations of Chinese women. The author reaches across continents, time, and tradition to find the path to acceptance and love.

Alice Walker's *The Color Purple* traces an abused woman's journey to the core of her own remarkable power. How did Walker's determined protagonist ever survive such a cruel assault?

And, finally, *Jubilee*, a remarkable epic by Margaret Walker, dramatizes the true story of the author's strong grandmother, Vyry—daughter of a house slave—and her master during the Civil War.

Happy reading!

Up Close and Personal with
Joyce Carol Thomas

———∿∿∿———

I must have fallen in love with words when I was still in the womb. Probably because my mother practically lived in the church house while she was pregnant with me.

In that little wooden white chapel on an Oklahoma hill, even the spoken words were sung with a kind of lilting sweetness, measured in breaths that rose and fell, words chanted back and forth from the preacher, the deacon, the mother of the church, and the female missionaries. In my writing, I try to re-create this music on the printed page. Sing the way those people used to sing.

My mother, Leona Haynes, was such an avid church-goer that one night while she was tarrying on the altar, our house burned down. She didn't get up off her knees to run and put out the fire or to try and save any of our worldly possessions. Maybe she already had the kind of fire described in the lyrics by the gospel quartet groups: "Holy Ghost, it's like fire shut up in my bones." She allowed life. She and my father built another house.

She told me that when she married my father, she owned a rag doll. My father threw the doll in the garbage can. "You want a baby girl, I'll give you a baby girl," he promised.

My mother gave birth to thirteen babies; nine of us lived. She kept having boys; she wanted a girl. I was fifth of the nine. And the first girl. My sister, Flora, born the year after me, was the second and last daughter. More brothers followed.

We lived in a small Oklahoma town called Ponca City. Although it was called Ponca City, it was no city. Its size at the time I lived there qualified it as a town. Still, the place was the world to me when I was young. It was only later that I understood, through comparison, what a quaint place Ponca City was.

Ponca City, as you know, is the setting for this book.

We stayed in Ponca until I was in the fourth grade.

Our Ponca house sat directly across the street from the school. Crispus Attucks School was named after the

African American hero, the first soldier to die in the Boston Massacre, 1770. My character Abyssinia Jackson attends a school with the same name.

Many readers have commented on the importance of food in my novels. Food, readers and reviewers say, occupies almost as much of a place as the book's setting. I suppose the food's joyous inclusion, a fragrant presence, comes from having a mother who was known as the best cook in town, and from having seven competing brothers and one cousin who staged eating contests. In my home, food was another language of love. In my novel *Marked by Fire*, broom wheat tea is steeped, poured, and sipped.

The small towns, the rural settings in which I grew up, have affected my life and my writing. I need and like open space. I like trees and flowers and the earth. And so do my characters. The cotton field in an important place for me, and for my *Marked by Fire* characters. Abyssinia is born in a cotton field very much similar to the one where my family and I worked during the summer and early autumn.

When we migrated to California, we moved again to a

small town setting in a rural area five miles out of Tracy. We continued to harvest crops, including tomatoes, yellow onions, strawberries, and the sweet black grapes of the San Joaquin Valley vineyards.

In contrast to our Ponca City school, where my classmates were all black, in our Tracy, California, one-room schoolhouse, there were only two African Americans: my sister and I. We looked forward to attending our little schoolhouse down the road. I was fascinated by and welcomed the likenesses and differences among ethnic groups different from mine.

Marked by Fire, my first novel, was written in Berkeley, California, where I still live. My Cedar Street home is a wonderful space in which to meditate and write. There are windows that open to generous light. The backyard is a mini-forest of pine, avocado, lemon, and fruit trees, with blackberry bushes gracing the landscape. I like to think I have the best of both worlds: my front windows look out onto the front yard and onto the street, with cars coming and going, with sidewalks leading to grocery stores, banks, the cleaners, and the post office. In my backyard, I treasure the country, and in my front yard, I enjoy the city.

Often one of the needs of a writer is the need to be alone. Some of my friends observe that I am alone even in a crowd of people. And that's probably true, too. I have to go inside myself in order to create. Yet I enjoy talking with students, teachers, librarians, booksellers, and readers of all generations and all cultures about my work. Perhaps I need the mountains and the multitudes.

For my entire life, my Aunt Corine, who was a respected Mother of her church, supported my need and passion for writing. She generously shared family history. She read all my drafts, laughed at the funny parts, and sighed at the sad passages. She lived to be ninety years old before she passed away on September 1, 2006. You will find that I acknowledge her in the front of this book for her unwavering support. I will continue to remember Mother Corine Coffey's wonderful spirit all the days of my life.